Wild Dust

The Musical

Music by
Dennis Poore

Book by
Flip Kobler & Cindy Marcus

Lyrics by
Flip Kobler

A Samuel French Acting Edition

SAMUEL
FRENCH
FOUNDED 1830
New York Hollywood London Toronto
SAMUELFRENCH.COM

ISBN 978-0-573-66391-8   Printed in U.S.A.   #29026

IMPORTANT BILLING AND CREDIT
REQUIREMENTS

WILD DUST THE MUSICAL was originally produced by Season Productions June 7 – June 23 at Centenary Stage Company in Hackettstown, New Jersey. The production was directed by Cindy Marcus, with musical direction by Fred Willard, choreography by Ann Barrett, scenic design by Flip Kobler, lighting design by Edward R. Matthews, sound design by Sarah Bader, and was produced by Kobbie Alamo with the following cast:

COOPER .... Christopher Chew
MARION.................................... Delana Hubscher
BELLE....................................... Jennifer Boutell
SALLY....................................... Nina Zoie Lam
DENISE...................................... Toni Lewis
HARD CORA................................ Angela Madaline
LOUISE STYLES .... Caroline Durham
GERTRUDE .... Elizabeth Cherry

For Kobbie Alamo

Who made it all real

(The fanfare hits and **COOPER** *steps out in front of the curtain. He's dressed all Roy Rogers-y right down to the silk bandanna and sequins. He pitches with full throttle energy.)*

Song - *WESTWARD BOUND*

COOPER.

GRAB YOUR HAT AND COME ON ALONG
WE'LL CHASE THE SUN ACROSS THE PLAINS
MOUNT UP YOUR SADDLE
ROUND UP YOUR CATTLE
JOIN US ON OUR WAGON TRAIN

WE'RE HEADING BACK TO THE FRONTIER
WHERE STRANGERS FLASH A FRIENDLY SMILE
BLUE SKIES WERE BLUER
TRUTH WAS TRUER
LEGENDS WERE NEWER AND BEGUILED
WHEN THE WEST WAS WILD

(A tumbleweed tumbles across stage.)

HI HO SILVER
LET'S GO WESTWARD
WHERE THERE'S ALWAYS A SHOWDOWN
JOIN THE STAMPEDE
'CROSS THE PRAIRIE
WHERE THE CAYOTES MAKE THEIR LONESOME
SOUND
WE'RE WESTWARD BOUND

(The curtains open to reveal our set. A large backdrop of an old western sunset hangs upstage. Stage left and right are teasers that hide the wings. The teasers are painted with huge, slightly skewed posters. Roy, Gene, Tex, Rex.)

(The girls from our cast are there, dressed in little Dale Evans outfits. Vests, matching skirts. Sequins. This is the cowgirl that never was.)

COOPER.
SHINE YER SPURS AND POINT THEM OUT WEST
BID YOUR TROUBLES

COOPER AND THE GIRLS.
ADIOS
LEAVE 'EM IN THE LOBBY
BE OUR KEMO SABE

COOPER.	THE GIRLS.
AND YOUR VIYAS WILL BE CONDIOSED	CONDIOSED
WILD DUST BLOWS THROUGH THE CANYONS	
CORRALS ARE BETTER THAN OKAY	AH-AHHHH
KAI-YAIS WERE YIPPEE'D	YIPPEE
HAWS WERE YE-E'D	YEE HAW
UPS WERE GIDDY'D IT'S TRUE	

COOPER AND THE GIRLS.
WHEN THE WEST WAS NEW

HI HO SILVER
LET'S GO WESTWARD
GOOD GUYS WEAR TEN GALLON CROWNS
LET'S GO YONDER
TO THE PONDER-
OSA THAT OASIS OUT OF TOWN
WE'RE WESTWARD BOUND

COOPER. Howdy folks, partners, buckaroos. You have all come to hear a story and I got one to tell. A genuine American folk tale. Well, more or less. So sit back, stick your tongue in your cheek, and hang on, cause Once Upon A Time… *(We hear the sound of the wind come up. Music does an ominous sting.)* The worst dust storm in a decade was about to hit our little town. Now the men had all left to drive the horses and cattle someplace safe to ride out the dust. Leaving the women to fend for themselves.

(Now one by one the girls come out of the wings to strut their stuff. **Costume note. All these women should be in their character costumes. But even these have a heightened reality. Still sequined and embroidered. Yokes and cuffs. They should all have that Saturday matinee feel.***)*

(Now there's also a **STAGEHAND** *here. This cowpoke will show up whenever needed to move furniture, hand over props, and do whatever is needed on this production.)*

COOPER. There you have it folks. You got four "ladies of the night" and three "ladies of the day" forced to bunk together for the next three days.

(The set is rolling into place from the wings. A back wall full of whiskey bottles covers up the western backdrop. A bar rolls in front of the back wall. A door slides in downstage left. Stairs sneak in stage right. A poker table and chairs come downstage right. The posters vanish. All this is butter smooth as **COOPER** *keeps talking.)*

COOPER. In the only building in town strong enough to withstand the pounding sand. The town brothel. Are you ready for a ride?

COOPER AND THE GIRLS.
LET'S GO WESTWARD
'CROSS THE DESERT
WHISKEY AND SALOON GIRLS ABOUND
FIND A TABLE
HEAR OUR FABLE
HAVE A LAUGH EXPECT NOTHING PROFOUND
WE'RE WESTWARD BOUND – YEE-HAW!

*(***COOPER** *comes forward and talks to the audience again.)*

COOPER. Well that's the nutshell of our little fable. But our story doesn't really begin until our dashing hero came staggering in, seeking shelter from the storm.

*(***COOPER** *vanishes into the wings. The wind picks up louder. A moment later he comes staggering in through the saloon door. Dust hammers in around him as he closes the door and looks to the audience..)*

COOPER. I know. I get to be the hero. HA!

> *(Then he's right back in character, coughing and hawkin' up sand when –)*

MARION. What's going on out there? *(Oh no.* **COOPER** *ducks behind the bar.)* Who's out there?

COOPER. *(Popping like a jack in the box)* Nobody! *(Whoops. Dang! He drops again.)*

MARION. You got to be somebody. *(She comes in with a gun.)*

COOPER. No I don't.

MARION. Yes you do.

COOPER. No I don't.

MARION. I got a gun.

COOPER. Me too. Colt.

MARION. Smith and Wesson Scofield.

COOPER. Whoa. *(He drops his gun on the bar and pops up, hands in the air.)* Big gun.

MARION. Damn right. Oh, shoot. *(She licks her fingers and smacks her wrist. Hard. He stares, dumbstruck.)* OW! I'm tryin' to quit cursin'. (**SALLY** *comes charging in with a frying pan screaming like a banshee, with* **BELLE** *on her heels.)*

SALLY. AHHHHHHHH! Sit!

COOPER. Okay. *(He drops out of sight behind the bar.)*

MARION. Get up.

COOPER. Okay. *(He pops up again.)*

BELLE. Hey that's a man.

SALLY. Gosh, are you sure, Belle?

> (**BELLE** *sticks out her tongue at* **SALLY**, *who tries to grab it. They both glare like rivaling sibs.)*

SALLY & BELLE. Grrrrrrrrr.

COOPER. Look ladies. I'm not lookin' for trouble. (**SALLY** *puts down the frying pan and scoops up* **COOPER**'*s gun.)* Hope he's not looking for me. I didn't know anybody was here. Wherever here is.

BELLE. Why, you're in a social club. You know, men come here to play some cards, have a drink and be *social.*

SALLY. What are you doin'?

BELLE. Bein' social.

SALLY. Fine. I'm Sally, this is Marion. The peach is Belle. Who are you?

COOPER. Nobody. Just your generic hero seeking shelter from the storm.

MARION. Well, Nobody, you can't stay.

COOPER. Why not?

SALLY. Ah…Rooms are a two hundred dollars a night.

COOPER. Big room is it?

SALLY. That's a special storm rate. A hundred and forty two percent inflation rate amortized over the length of the storm. You got two hundred dollars?

COOPER. You can't send me out there. I'm on foot.

BELLE. Where's your horse?

COOPER. Dead. *(The women gasp in shock.)*

SALLY. Where's your sidekick?

COOPER. Don't have one. *(The women gasp harder.)*

SALLY. You don't have a horse. Or a sidekick? What kind of hero are you?

COOPER. Average kind. *(To avoid further questions he takes a sip from a canteen on the bar.)*

SALLY. That our water? Twenty two ninety five!

COOPER. What?

SALLY. The water. Twenty two dollars and ninety five cents. It's a special –.

COOPER & SALLY. Storm rate.

COOPER. Right.

BELLE. Here, take some whiskey. Martin won't care. Not anymore.

*(She almost laughs. **MARION** and **SALLY** stomp and glare daggers at her. **COOPER** takes the bottle she offers and drains about half.)*

COOPER. Who's Martin?

BELLE. Oh, he's the body –

MARION. No body! Nobody. He's nobody. Different nobody. The bartender. He's the bartender here. *(***COOPER** *looks to the "M" over the bar and* **MARION** *jumps in with –)* The M stands for Marion's place. That's me. Marion. My place. Heluva name huh? Oh shoot. *(She tugs a hair out of her head.)* Ow.

COOPER. Well ladies, pleasure is mine. You take your water, I'll take my gun and –

SALLY. *(Almost does it, then thinks better of it.)* No.

COOPER. What?

SALLY. We don't know who you are. I'm sure not going to give you a gun.

BELLE. But it's HIS gun.

SALLY. Yeah, but we don't know anything about him.

COOPER. Nothin' to know. I'm just a mysterious stranger.

MARION. We had lots of mysterious strangers ride through. They all had horses.

BELLE. And sidekicks.

SALLY. Except the bad guys.

COOPER. I'm not a bad guy.

SALLY. Who else would be running in a storm except an outlaw?

COOPER. I'm not an outlaw.

MARION. Then who are you?

COOPER. *(To the audience.)* See, this is where it started to go bad for me. I *really* didn't want them to know who I was. But I needed my gun. But to get my gun I had to tell them who I was. See my problem? So I did the honorable thing…I lied. *(He strikes a pose. The* **STAGE-HAND** *leans out and hands him a guitar that just happens to match his sequined outfit.)*

Song - NOBODY

I'M JUST THE NAMELESS COWBOY OF THE OLD WILD WEST
A PHANTOM OF THE PLAINS
THE FACELESS STRANGER RIDING IN THE SUNSET
WITHOUT A WHISPER OF A NAME

MARION, BELLE & SALLY.
>AHH-OOOOOM.

COOPER.
>I'M A LEGEND OF THE PRAIRIE
>THE MYTH THE FAIRYTALE
>I HEED THE CALL OF THE DESERT
>AND THE GENERIC TRAIL

MARION, BELLE & SALLY.
>AHH-OOOOOM. AHH-OOOOOM

COOPER
>MY NAME IS NOBODY-YODEL-DE-DO-YODEL-DI DOH
>LIKE A TUMBLEWEED I ROAM
>WHITE KNIGHT'LL-IT'LL-IDLE IDLE IDLE DE DO
>GOT NO PLACE TO CALL HOME
>ON THE HORIZON THERE'S A SUNSET WAITING FOR ME
>>I'M A ONE MAN POSSE IN SEARCH OF MY DESTINY
>I RIDE WITH THE DAWN AND KEEP NO COMPANY
>>I GOTTA GODLE-DE-DO-DODLE-TOOTLE-LOO
>MY NAME IS NOBODY

COOPER. *(To the audience.)* You know I was fixin' to leave right then, gun or not. Probably would have. Except for one thing.

(He opens the door and dust pounds in. Wind howls. He slams the door shut again.)

COOPER. I didn't know the storm had gotten that bad. Now I wasn't scared exactly, I just figured It'd be better if I just hunkered down here until the storm passed. You know, protect the women. And the girls seemed thrilled with that.

*(**MARION**, **SALLY** and **BELLE** shove him toward the door.)*

MARION, BELLE & SALLY.
>YOU KNOW WE'RE THRILLED TO MEET YA
>BUT WE DON'T WANNA KEEP YA
>FEEL FREE TO COME AGAIN
>DROP A LINE SOON AS YOU CAN
>GOODBYE NOW – HAPPY TRAILS TO YA PARD

(**SALLY** *actually gives him back his gun and tries to shove him out the door.* **COOPER** *ain't leaving.*)

COOPER.	MARION, BELLE & SALLY.
I GOT NO WHERE TO GO I'M LEFT WITHOUT A HORSE	
WHAT'S THE RUSH ANYWAY	YOU COULD WALK TO DODGE BY SUNRISE
I'M A PEOPLE PERSON SOCIAL ANIMAL	
WE DON'T COME ALONG EVERY DAY	YOU BETTER GET A MOVE ON BEFORE THE WIND GETS TOO STRONG
A MAN NEEDS HIM A BUNKHOUSE	GOODBYE
WHERE HE CAN STAY IN ANONYMITY	SO LONG
A CASTLE ON THE RANGE	SEE YA
WITH A PRINCESS AS COMPANY	WHY ARE YOU STILL AROUND
AH-OOOOM	AH-OOOOM
I THINK I'LL STAY-DEL-DE DO-YODEL-DE-DO- YODEL-DI DOH	
AND COOL MY HEELS A SPELL	AND HOW WE WISH YOU COULD STAY
STAKE A CLAIM'LL DEEDLE DIDLE	YOU SHOULD GO

ALL.

WHILE/BEFORE THE SKY UNLEASHES HELL

MARION, BELLE & SALLY.	COOPER.
ON THE HORIZON THERE'S A SUNSET WAITING FOR YOU	THE SUN WON'T MIND IF I'M LATE
SOMEWHERE THE PRAIRIE IS WAITIN' TO RENDEZVOUS	THE PRAIRIE WILL HAVE TO WAIT

BE THE TUMBLEWEED	THIS TUMBLEWEED
YOU ARE AND	AIN'T GONNA STRAY
VAMOOSE TO LANDS	
FAR AWAY	
YOU SHOULD	I THINK THAT I'M
SKEEDATTLE-DE-DO-	GONNA STAY
DODLE-DE-DO-DO	
WHOEVER YOU ARE	

ALL.

WHILE THE STORM RAGES ON THIS AIN'T NO/WILL
BE MY SANCTUARY
AIN'T NO/PERFECT REFUGE OO-DOODLE AH
DOODLE.
FOR NOBODY

COOPER.

AND I'LL TELL YA THAT MY NAME IS NOBODY

*(He strikes a hero's pose. The girls collapse on the table in defeat. He's not leaving. Just then **DENISE** comes rushing out, blindly slamming into **COOPER**. They find themselves in each other's arms. He likes what he sees. She just goes panic-rigid. The other girls nearly freak.)*

COOPER. Well howdy.

DENISE. Erp!

COOPER. Who are you? *(She recoils like he was a rattler. The girls swarm in front of her again, protecting her.)*

MARION. This here's Denise. She's ah –

SALLY. Yes she is. She's a –

MARION. Yeah. Yeah, she's ah –

BELLE. Not very sociable.

MARION & SALLY. Right!

COOPER. *(To the audience)* Did you get that the girls were hiding something? Cause I didn't have a clue.

HARD CORA. *(offstage)* Thought I heard singin'. This a party?

(She comes down the stairs.)

MARION. Sorry Cora. Did we wake you? We'll keep it down. Go to sleep.

HARD CORA. Who's the cowboy?

BELLE. Nobody.

HARD CORA. Named after yer pa, were ya? *(COOPER can't help but smile, he likes her. They shake. She's got a grip like a lumberjack.)* They call me Hard Cora. 'Lo!

MARION. Cora's our local blacksmith. She's hell with a hammer. Shoot! *(She bites a knuckle.)* Ow!

> *(LOUISE STYLES comes plodding down, grumpy and out of sorts. It's amazing how she can manage to look down her nose at everyone at the same time. Her daughter GERT is in tow on an invisible leash, both dressed in matching nightgowns and bonnets. COOPER drinks some more.)*

LOUISE STYLES. Would anyone like to articulate what's going on out here? I'm in my room trying to get some rest and you're all out here reveling in some Bacchanalian party. Who is this?

SALLY. Says his name's nobody.

LOUISE STYLES. That's not a name.

BELLE. Actually, it's Nobody-dodeldeedoo. *(That conspiratorial whisper.)* I think he's Swedish.

LOUISE STYLES. Your name sir?

COOPER. Hey, a rose by any other name –

LOUISE STYLES. Is still called something. What do we call you?

HARD CORA. What are you so afraid of?

COOPER. *(Quickly.)* Cooper. *(Uh-oh. Before anymore questions –)* Just call me Cooper.

LOUISE STYLES. Mister Cooper. People call me Missus Henry David Styles. And this is my daughter…

> *(But GERT is wandering around, taking in all the sights around her. Here she is, trapped in a brothel in a dust storm with a strange cowboy. She looks scared and lost.)*

LOUISE STYLES. Gertrude. Come here. My daughter Gertrude. Close your robe Gert.

COOPER. Gertrude. Something wrong?

GERTIE. No. I'm sorry…I didn't meant to stare…You know what I mean. I just –I'm not –

LOUISE STYLES. She's been away at school. Hasn't seen a cowboy in some time.

COOPER. School? Huh. So, you don't actually work here?

(HA! **CORA** *brays a snort of laughter.* **LOUISE** *gets deeply offended.)*

HARD CORA. No, we don't work here. No offense Marion. We'se just here cause of the storm.

COOPER. Me too.

LOUISE STYLES. Well isn't that fine. *(He drinks from the bottle again.)* Then get him a glass. You girls can still fake manners, can't you? You fake everything else. Isn't this wonderful, Gert? To have a man to offer us his sword and armor. My Henry wanted to stay and protect us himself. But he had a duty to lead the other men with the horses and cattle. He owns the livery you know.

MARION. And the mercantile.

HARD CORA. And the bank.

COOPER. Sounds like quite a man.

LOUISE STYLES. Oh he is. He tried to put us on a stage-coach. But we don't run from our troubles, do we Gert? So here we are.

MARION. Yup, here we all are. Now that you've met everybody I'm sure you're anxious to be on your way.

LOUISE STYLES. What? Where are you going?

COOPER. Where *am* I going?

MARION. Don't know, but no sense in being late.

LOUISE STYLES. Nonsense. A gentleman would never abandon a lady in distress!

HARD CORA. HA! We don't need him.

LOUISE STYLES. Obviously you know nothing about a dust storm –

HARD CORA. Danged if I don't. I saw one once when I'se a kid. Dust blew so hard and fast it blasted down everything in its path. Lasted four days and leveled every wooden building for ten miles. I saw it take a full grown steer down layer by layer. First its skin peeled off like a banana, then muscle, then it spread its guts to the horizon, while the bull bellowed into the wind.

(Beat. Everyone's looking at her, jaws on the floor, eyes wide in terror. Beat. Then –)

HARD CORA. What?

MARION. *(Pulling* **COOPER** *to his feet)* Well then you're gonna want to hurry, Sweetie.

LOUISE STYLES. *(Pulling him back into the chair)* He can't leave.

MARION. He can't stay. *(Yanking him up and pushing toward the door.)*

COOPER. Ladies.

LOUISE STYLES. *(Yanking him from the door.* **COOPER***'s passed around like pinball.)* Is this what you call hospitality?

MARION. No, I call it a door.

COOPER. Ladies.

LOUISE STYLES. We may need him.

HARD CORA. HA!

COOPER. Ladies!

GERTIE. Mother.

LOUISE STYLES. *(Not now)* Gert.

BELLE. Marion.

MARION. *(Not now)* Belle.

COOPER. Ladies!!!

ALL THE WOMEN. WHAT?!

(Instead of answering, he collapses in a dead faint. Outta here. The girls just watch him topple to the floor. They all stand a moment, wondering what to do next.)

DENISE. Erp.

SALLY. So…what now?

MARION. Now we got trouble.

(Blackout)

Scene 2

(The wind whips up even louder. **COOPER** *gets to his feet in the blackout and again comes forward to yak at us.)*

COOPER. Okay, first of all, I did *not* pass out from the whiskey. Let's be clear on that. It was…fatigue. But I was there to stay. Belle and Sally were wrestlin' me into a bunk when this happened a little while later. If I hadn't been asleep upstairs, I woulda found out what the girls were hidin'.

(A light comes up on **DENISE** *sitting in the corner, shaking all over. When the stage goes to full light,* **MARION** *pours a cup of coffee and leaves the pot behind the bar. She takes the cup to* **DENISE**, *soothing like a red hen.)*

MARION. It's alright. It's okay darlin'. Everything's going to be fine. Take a sip. Just a little one. How are you feelin'? Denise honey?

*(***BELLE** *enters from the bedrooms, wiping her hands on a towel.* **SALLY** *follows.)*

BELLE. Well, he's still out. He's either dead tired or dead drunk.

SALLY. Or just dead. *(They look at her.)* Hey, he weighed a ton.

MARION. So who is he?

SALLY. No idea, but he can pay for a room. *(She fans a wad of bills.)* He's got over three hundred dollars on him.

BELLE. You went through his pockets? Why didn't you just cheat it out of him like you do everybody else?

SALLY. For the last time Belle, I don't cheat. And I didn't go through his pockets. I was tryin' to find out who he is. See if he had any identification. The money fell out.

MARION. This has been one hell of a night. Shoot! *(She stomps on her own toe!)* Ow! Maybe we should just get this done before things get worse. C'mon girls.

*(***SALLY** *and* **BELLE** *schlump past like chastised children going to the woodshed. They Exit.* **DENISE** *doesn't want*

to go. But wrestles up the courage and does. From off-stage we hear MOANS. Sexual ecstasy?)

*(Nope. Cause two seconds later they come in with a dead body in tow. **MARTIN** the bartender. His shirt is stained red in front. They're struggling under the weight of the poor guy, staggering like Moe, Larry and Curly. **MARTIN** wears only one boot.)*

SALLY. I was wrong about Cooper. This is really dead weight.

DENISE. *(panicing and droping her end.)* Wait, this is wrong. I can't do this.

MARION. Can we discuss this later?

DENISE. No, we shouldn't be doing this.

BELLE. Maybe she's right.

SALLY. Oh please. When did you get scruples?

BELLE. What's that mean? Is that an insult. *(dropping her end of the body)* Marion do I have scruples?

MARION. Ladies, knock it off. Let's get him outside.

DENISE. Aren't we at least going to give him a decent burial?

*(**SALLY** goes to talk to **DENISE**, leaving **MARION** holding the body all alone. She starts to sink under the weight of it. A slow elevator to the floor.)*

SALLY. You want to spend an hour outside in that? No. You heard Cora. We just dump his body outside in the storm and let the dust eat away the evidence.

DENISE. That's inhuman.

SALLY. So was he. The man was a pimp, bully, drunk, horse thief, and a murdering rapist. He was evil through and through. You know that.

DENISE. I know. But maybe there was a little bit of good in him. I mean the bible says...

Song - LITTLE BIT OF GOOD

DENISE. *(Standing over him like delivering last rites.)*
THERE'S A LITTLE BIT OF GOOD IN EVERYBODY
MAYBE THERE'S A GEM DEEP IN HIS SOUL
WHAT IF THERE'S SOME GOOD IN THAT BODY
WE JUST DIDN'T DIG DEEP FOR THE GOLD

*(***MARION** *and* **SALLY** *lock eyes. The music kicks up and –)*

MARION. Doll, if we could dig that deep, we'd be in Shanghai. He had no soul. Remember…

                    SALLY & BELLE.

YOU CANNOT IGNORE
– IT'S HAPPENED
BEFORE
HE RIPPED A WOMAN'S   OH THE SHAME
PRIDE TO SHAME
BUT FOR GOD'S SAVING
GRACE –
THAT WAS US IN YOUR
PLACE
WE'D HAVE DONE THE   DONE THE SAME DONE
SAME   THE SAME
IT'S A SERVICE TO
MANKIND
SAYETH THE LORD,
BABY, "VENGEANCE IS
MINE."
WE DID WHAT WE
MUST – TIME FOR DUST
INTO DUST
THE TRUTH SHALL SET
US FREE

MARION. So we just get him outside and let God make the judgment.

DENISE. But what about us? What'll God say about what we're doin'?
WE'LL BURN IN HELL

MARION.
> GOD WON'T DO THAT TO US

DENISE.
> HOW CAN YOU TELL

MARION.
> CAUSE IT'S IN GOD WE TRUST
> AND WE HAVE FAITH
> THAT HE CAN SEE OUR SOUL AND KNOW....   KNOW
>   KNOW

MARION, BELLE AND SALLY.
> THERE'S A LITTLE BIT OF GOOD IN EVERYBODY
> WE'RE JUST ACTIN' IN OUR OWN DEFENSE
> LITTLE BIT OF GOOD IN EVERYBODY
> I KNOW HE'LL BELIEVE OUR INNOCENCE

SALLY. But we gotta move fast while we've got the chance.

MARION. And we gotta do this together. What do you say Doll?

MARION, BELLE AND SALLY.
> STAND WITH US SISTER
> TOGETHER WE'VE BEEN THROUGH BOTH THICK
> AND THIN
> STAND WITH US SISTER
> YOU'VE GOT TO CHOOSE BETWEEN US OR HIM
> STAND WITH US SISTER

MARION.
> WE'LL DO WHATEVER YOU DECIDE....

SALLY.
> YOU DECIDE

BELLE.
> YOU DECIDE

DENISE.	MARION, BELLE AND SALLY.
OOOOOOH, LET'S DO	LET'S DO WHAT'S
WHAT'S GOOD	GOOD
FOR EVERYBODY	GOTTA DO WHAT'S
	BEST FOR ALL
WE CAN'T UNDO	AND YOU KNOW THE
WHAT'S ALREADY BEEN	DEED'S BEEN DONE
DONE	

GOTTA DO WHAT'S GOOD	DOIN' WHAT'S GOOD
FOR EVERYBODY	FOR EVERYONE

ALL 4 GIRLS.
IT'S ONE FOR ALL, WE'RE STANDING ALL FOR ONE

MARION, BELLE & SALLY. **DENISE.**

THERE'S A LITTLE BIT OF GOOD	LITTLE BIT OF GOOD
IN EVERYBODY	IN EVERYBODY
THERE'S A SPARK OF WARMTH	
IN OUR POOR TRAMPLED HEARTS	OUR POOR TRAMPLED HEARTS
LITTLE BIT OF GOOD	LITTLE BIT OF GOOD
IN EVERYBODY	

ALL FOUR GIRLS.
THIS IS A CHANCE FOR A BRAND NEW START
AMEN. Halleluiah.

(Music out. They move to hoist the body. They lose control and end up with him draped over the bar. That's when they notice –)

MARION. Where's his other...ah...

SALLY. Boot.

MARION. Yeah.

(They all start looking. Frantically.)

MARION. We have to find it before someone else does. They'll ask questions if they find only one boot. Who wears one boot?

BELLE. Pirates.

(They start ad-libbing in their panic to find the missing boot. **BELLE**, **DENISE** *and* **SALLY** *fade into the kitchen, leaving* **MARION** *to search around out here.)*

(That's when **MRS. HENRY DAVID STYLES** *can be heard sneezing off stage. She's heading this way. Oh Geez, she's headin' this way. Panic. Seconds now. Maybe less. What to do?)*

(MARION just shoves the body and it topples with a THUD behind the bar, just a nanosecond before LOUISE and GERT clomp in. So to cover the noise, MARION coughs loudly, banging on the bar. LOUISE and GERT are carrying a huge wedding quilt between them.)

GERTIE. Are you alright?

MARION. Me? Oh yes. Thank you. I'm perfect. I have a little hang-nail, but other than that, I'm dandy. Go back to sleep.

LOUISE STYLES. No, we'd like some coffee, please. Cream and sugar. *(She sits at the table like this was a fine restaurant.)*

MARION. Excuse me?

LOUISE STYLES. Coffee. The drink made from beans. I'm sure you've heard of it.

MARION. I'm not a maid. What do I look like to you?

LOUISE STYLES. *(Long deadpan. Answer enough.)* Fine. Gertrude, get us some coffee please. *(And GERT starts walking toward –)* Mugs are behind the bar.

MARION. The bar?! No. I'll get it. Sit. I'll get it. *(She grabs two mugs from behind the bar.)*

LOUISE STYLES. Gertrude, sit down. **(GERT** *does as* **MARION** *comes up with the coffee.* **LOUISE** *begins to quilt.* **CORA** *comes down the stairs.)*

HARD CORA. Morning everyone. *(She starts for the bar when–)*

MARION. CORA!

HARD CORA. *(Yikes)* What?!

MARION. Morning Cora. Whatcha doin'?

HARD CORA. Uh-huh. Mornin'. Coffee looks good. Getting' me a mug.

MARION. I'll get it.

HARD CORA. Marion, you don't have to wait on me.

MARION. I don't mind. Sit.

(So she sits. **CORA** *goes to get another mug from behind the bar.* **CORA** *takes out some chaw, puts a pinch between her cheek and gum and offers it up to* **LOUISE.** *)*

HARD CORA. Care for some?

LOUISE STYLES. Hmph. *(So* **CORA** *offers some to* **GERT** *who goes to reach for it. Louse slaps her hand.)* Try it and I'll die of shame and take you with me.

*(***MARION** *comes back with the mug as* **COOPER** *comes down, heading for the bar.* **MARION** *stops him)*

COOPER. Morning everyone.

LOUISE STYLES. Good morning, Mister Cooper.

MARION. Doesn't anybody sleep?! Go back to bed.

COOPER. Sorry, I just need a little hair of the dog. *(He tries again,* **MARION** *stops him again.)*

MARION. There's no hair. There's no dog. I have allergies.

COOPER. Coffee then?

MARION. I'll get you a mug.

(She forces **COOPER** *to sit next to* **GERT** *and goes to get another mug from behind the bar.)*

COOPER. That wind sure is howlin'. Think it's gonna crack it's cheeks?

HARD CORA. *(Ominous as hell.)* It'll get worse yet. Louder. Faster. Until you think hell herself has come to skin you alive and grind your soul into grit —*(She notices the terrified looks.)* What?

*(***MARION** *jams the mug in front of him. Pours the coffee. He tries to stand, she forces him down and turns his head to face* **GERTRUDE**, *about 3 inches from her face.)*

COOPER. So. You said you been away at school.

GERTIE. Yeah. St. Catherine's. That's a Catholic…well what I mean is…Um, you know…only girls…not many, ah… Well, you know what I mean.

LOUISE STYLES. No Gertrude. Articulate. Gentlemen like women who can express themselves.

GERTIE. *(Deadpan.)* Private school.

COOPER. So, you planning on more education?

LOUISE STYLES. No, it's a finishing school. Once done she'll be finished.

HARD CORA. Finished what?

LOUISE STYLES. She'll have the proper skills to be a lady. Attract a suitable man like my Henry. *(She shows off her pearl necklace.)* These were a gift for our last anniversary. One pearl for every year we've been married. Extravagant, but he's a born romantic. Watch your stitches, Gertrude, eleven stitches to the inch.

GERTIE. Yes momma.

COOPER. Hey, this is kinda nice. *(He studies the quilt)*

LOUISE STYLES. It's Gertrude's wedding quilt.

> *(**COOPER** drops the quilt as if it were on fire. He stands and heads for the bar. Now each person stands, forcing **MARION** to wrestle each person back to their seats. Like those guys in the circus that keep all those plates spinning.)*

MARION. What?

COOPER. Just wanted some sugar.

MARION. All we have is honey. And we're out of honey. What?

GERTIE. My mother wants some cream.

MARION. The cow's in some cave by now. What?!

> *(**HARD CORA** grabs the spittoon from near the bar. **MARION** gets them all back to the table –)*

MARION. SIT!

> *(They all do. Just then **MARTIN** comes falling out from behind the bar. Ah! **MARION** runs to drag him back into hiding. **COOPER** shifts uneasily at something in his hip pocket. He reaches in and pulls out a tattered book and sets it on the table. **LOUISE** looks at it and is even more impressed.)*

LOUISE STYLES. Edgar Allen Poe. You're an educated man. Where did you attend school?

COOPER. Hard Knocks U.

LOUISE STYLES. And you've never been married?

COOPER. No. Been waitin' for the right calico angel. I figure when I meet the right girl my whole world will be a love song.

LOUISE STYLES. Oh, I know exactly how you feel. But you need to act now. My mother always said dreams don't come true unless you work for them. I keep telling this one, find a man while you're still young. I keep trying to teach her to cook. She's trying, she'll get it some day, won't you Gert?

GERTIE. I suppose so.

LOUISE STYLES. You just need to put a bit more effort into it. Eleven stitches Gertrude. Eleven. That's how you make something last. *(She rises and puts the quilt on the bar,* **MARION** *trying to block her view. Before* **LOUISE** *can get too suspicious –)*

GERTIE. What if that's not –I mean what if I don't –What if

LOUISE STYLES. Don't waver Gertrude. Be sure of yourself.

GERTIE. What if I was to say I'm not sure I want to get married.

LOUISE STYLES. Of course you want to get married.

GERTIE. I do?

LOUISE STYLES. See, you've already got your speech prepared. Oh Gertrude, marriage is the most perfect of God's institutions.

HARD CORA. Hah!

LOUISE STYLES. Perhaps you'll understand that someday dear. To finally become a Missus is the day all girls dream of. A feeling you'll never forget. How can I explain it?

(And on that cue the **STAGEHAND** *comes out with an old '40's microphone. WDST is emblazoned across it.* **STAGE-HAND** *sets it so* **LOUISE** *can sing like Patsy Cline.)*

Song - MAN BY YOUR SIDE

LOUISE STYLES.

HE CAME WALKIN' FROM THE SUNSET THAT EVENIN'
LIKE A PRINCE IN SOME DREAM FAIRYLAND
KNELT ON THE PORCH BEHIND TWO DOZEN ROSES
AND ASKED MY DADDY FOR MY HAND

WITH A MAN BY MY SIDE
I STOOD AT THE ALTER

NEATH THE STAINED GLASS AND PEAR BLOSSOM
STRANDS
I FEEL MY HEART AGLOW
CAUSE I KNOW
MY FUTURE'S
GONNA FLOW OVER WITH JOY
AS I SLIP ON THAT LITTLE GOLD BAND

HARD CORA. Interestin' perspective.

LOUISE STYLES. I don't expect *you* to understand. Being a single…*(searching for the word…)* … girl. It's different –

HARD CORA. I was married once.

GERTIE. Really?

LOUISE STYLES. Really?

COOPER. Really?

HARD CORA. Yeah!. And I gotta tell ya, my marriage sorta lacked that romantic rosey glow.

*(And now the **STAGEHAND** is there with a matching microphone. It's dueling Patsy's –)*

HE BEAT ME THE FIRST TIME ON OUR WEDDIN'
NIGHT
BROKE MY COLLAR AND TWO FINGERS ON MY HAND
HE GOT TO LIKE IT AND DONE IT BOUT FOUR TIMES
A WEEK
TILL I COCKED HIM WITH MY FRYIN' PAN

SO I STOOD BY MY MAN
TILL HE WAS SLEEPIN'
THEN I TENDERLY BROKE BOTH OF HIS KNEES
I WON'T LIVE IN FEAR
WHEN I HEAR
HIS FOOTSTEPS
APPROACHING NEAR IN THE DARK
CAUSE HE COULDN'T WALK FOR NEARLY TWELVE
WEEKS.

GERTIE. You left your husband? Wow. *(This is unheard of to* **GERT**.*)*

HARD CORA. Good thing too.

LOUISE STYLES. It's not good. You broke a vow. A promise to God.

HARD CORA. I had no choice.

LOUISE STYLES. But a *lady* always will. Which is what I'm
trying to teach you Gertrude.

TAME A LION WITH A GENTLE DEMEANOR

HARD CORA.

HIS DEMEANOR CAN GET MEANER YET

LOUISE STYLES.

MAKE A HOME OF CHIFFON AND A BEDROOM OF
LACE

HARD CORA.

KEEP A GUN IN YOUR APRON POCKET

BOTH.

WITH A MAN BY YOUR SIDE

YOU'RE SAFE AND PROTECTED

LOUISE STYLES. Finally we agree.

HARD CORA.

HE CAN'T SWING HARD IF YOU'RE IN HIS ARMS

LOUISE STYLES.

A WOMAN MUST SOFTEN HIM

REFORM HIM

BRING OUT HIS

FEMININE SIDE WITH A SMILE

HARD CORA.

IF THAT FAILS A POT WORKS LIKE A CHARM

BOTH.

DON'T YOU REALIZE

THAT'S THE LIFE

A YOUNG AND

DOTING WIFE SURE CAN EXPECT

LOUISE STYLES.

FROM HER LOVING MAN

HARD CORA.

WHO NEEDS A LOVING MAN

GERTIE. WHO NEEDS A LOVING MAAAaaaaaann-gh-
ahem.

(As the song ends. **COOPER** *vanishes. The* **STAGEHAND**
takes the microphones offstage. **LOUISE** *is pissed.)*

LOUISE STYLES. I'll thank you to keep your opinions to yourself.

HARD CORA. I just thought Gert there deserved another perspective.

LOUISE STYLES. I think I know what's best for my daughter. I don't need you filling her head with a passel of lies.

HARD CORA. They ain't lies Missus Style. It's what happened to me.

LOUISE STYLES. But it won't happen to her. She's not like you. I mean look at you. Is it any wonder he treated you like a common ranch hand. Come along Gertrude, I don't want you listening to this.

(She pounds upstairs leaving silence in her wake. GERTIE musters her courage and walks to CORA...)

GERTIE. I believe you.

LOUISE STYLES. Gertrude, now! And bring your quilt.

(GERT shrugs helplessly at CORA, then turns and marches to the bar, reaching over to grab the quilt. She GASPS. MARION pops up like a jack-in-the-box, holding one of MARTIN's arm's that sticks up like a tree branch. MARION GASPS. Both look to the MARTIN's arm. Both GASP! MARION shoves the arm down. Shock-freeze. Neither moves. Both women stare at each other, a whole conversation going on between their eyes. Then GERT turns zombie-like and staggers toward the stairs while MARION swallows her heart.)

GERTIE. Excuse me. I just have to... my mother may need... pardon me.

(And she's gone leaving CORA to stare at the floor in doubt. She looks at her calloused hands...)

HARD CORA. I've known some good ranch hands. Haven't you?

MARION. Sure.

HARD CORA. Yeah. Sure. Nothin' wrong with that. 'Scuse me.

(CORA heads upstairs. SALLY, BELLE and DENISE come poking back in. To SALLY and DENISE –)

MARION. You find that boot. Belle, let's get him hidden again until we can find the stupid thing. *(MARION and BELLE wrestle him back into the kitchen.)*

DENISE. This is really happening isn't it? Can we make this not be real? Close the book and pretend? Let's go back to yesterday. Or Tuesday. Tuesday was a good day.

SALLY. Shh-sh-sh. Until we get Martin outside it's better if you don't talk. Not in your condition. Not a word to anybody. Not a peep. Not a sound. Alright? *(DENISE nods.)* Promise? *(DENISE nods again.)* Promise you won't talk? *(Another nod.)* You got to say I promise.

DENISE. I promise.

SALLY. Shh. Not a sound. Didn't I just say that? Gee-whiz. Find that boot. I'll look upstairs.

(She vanishes upstairs. DENISE is looking for a boot. She finds the book COOPER left on the table. She starts to leaf through it. She's intrigued when COOPER comes back in.)

COOPER. Oh howdy!

DENISE. AHHHHHHHHHHHH!

(Startled, she screams, which freaks COOPER. He instantly wheels around, instinctively pulling for his gun that isn't there. A gun fighter reacting on feral blood. He holds the pose a moment, then realizes his body language may be giving too much away. He tries to play it cool.)

COOPER. Ha. Didn't mean to scare you. You kinda scared me though, huh? You don't talk much do ya? *(She turns and tries to run upstairs.)* Hey wait. *(She stops and spins, clutching that book to her chest.)* Is that my book? *(She comes down and tries to hand it to him while standing ten feet away.)* It's okay, I didn't mean… *(She won't look at him, just holds it out. Her hand shakes a lot.)* You're trembling. You like books? *(She does)* Yeah. They got a way of kinda sandin' down the rougher edges on life. Does that make sense or am I an idiot? *(She nods emphatically.)* I'm an idiot? *(She shakes a hard NO.)* This one here's by a fellah named Edgar Allen Poe. He's got a poem in here... Here it is. "It was many and many a year ago in a Kingdom by the sea. That a maiden there lived whom you may know by the name of Annabel Lee. And this maiden she lived with no other thought than to love. And to be loved by me."

*(He turns to face her and we hear a love song. **COOPER** has found his soul mate. He turns to the audience and smiles.)*

Isn't that something? *(Then back to **DENISE**.)* You can borrow it if you want. Heck, you can have it.

*(The moment heats – until **SALLY** comes rushing in. She carries the damn lost boot. She sees **COOPER** talking to **DENISE** and glowers. **DENISE** tries to hide behind the book.)*

SALLY. Oh no.

COOPER. Morning miss Sally.

SALLY. *(Spinning in the door, the boot hidden out of sight. She thinks at warp speed.)* Morning. Hey, you wanna give me a hand. Once of the shutters came free and the storm is rippin' through your bedroom.

*(He trots off to fix it, **SALLY** on his heels. **DENISE** takes a beat, then follows just as **MARION** and **BELLE** come plodding back in. **SALLY** comes sneaking back....)*

MARION. It's got to be somewhere. What's that noise?

SALLY. I opened a window.

MARION. In a storm?

SALLY. I had to. He was *talking to Denise.*

MARION. We gotta keep him away from her.

SALLY. I found the boot.

MARION. That's great, Doll. Where?

SALLY. In *his* room. But while I was in there, his saddle bags, you know, just happened to be open –

BELLE. How much does he have?

SALLY. Another two hundred and fifty dollars.

MARION. That's a lot of money.

BELLE. You think he's a bank robber?

SALLY. Worse. He has a badge. He could be a U.S. Marshall.

(Beat while the weight of that sinks in.)

BELLE. Now we got trouble.

(BLACKOUT)

Scene 3

(The lights come up and **COOPER** *talks excitedly to us again.)*

COOPER. Maybe this was my chance. Nobody knew who I was. Maybe I could make a clean start. I was smitten. I wanted to know everything about her. Everything. Including her limited vocabulary. Well, I had a plan to find out.

(The lights come up on the poker table while **SALLY** *sottos to* **BELLE**.*)*

SALLY. We got to find out if this man really is a Marshal. It's gotta be done real subtle, so you just let me do the talking.

COOPER. *(Joining them at the table.)* Okay ladies, the game is five card stud. So, tell me about Denise.

BELLE. Well she was born in Wyoming, wanted to be a teacher –

SALLY. Shut up Belle.

COOPER. Has she never been able to talk?

BELLE. Oh no, that didn't start until recent. Sally told her to –

SALLY. Shut up Belle.

BELLE. Speakin' of recent, you ever had any *other* jobs recently? Maybe in "law enforcement" or something –

SALLY. Shut up Belle.

COOPER. Where's she from?

SALLY. Where are you from?

BELLE. Well I'm from –

SALLY. Shut up Belle. Where are *you* from?

COOPER. Either of you ever been to San Francisco? *(Nope.)* Then that's where I'm from.

BELLE. Really? Do you know Westley Barker?

SALLY. Not again.

BELLE. Tall. Dark hair. Dreamy eyes. And a little drawl like mine?

COOPER. Friend of yours?

BELLE. Fiancé. We left Atlanta together. We got this far before someone ruined our life. *(She flicks* **SALLY***'s ear.)* Sally tricked him into a poker game and cheated him out of all our money.

SALLY. I don't cheat.

BELLE. Left us penniless. He had to go on alone to get us a stake. Set up shop. He's a newspaper man. Yes sir, he's coming back for me and I'm going to live happily ever after as Mrs. Beaufort Westley Barker.

SALLY. Three deuces.

COOPER. Damn. So what *can* you tell me about Denise?

BELLE. Well she –

SALLY. I'm thinking of having "Shut up Belle" tattooed on my forehead to save time. We can't tell you anything. She's a recluse. Never talks. Like a hermit.

COOPER. *(Standing.)* I guess I better get it from the horse's mouth.

SALLY. NO! Ah... You should probably stay away. She's contagious.

BELLE. She is? *(***SALLY*** elbows her in the guts.* **BELLE** *gets the ploy and jumps right in embellishing.)* She is. Disfiguring disease. Horrible purple rash. Clashes with everything she wears.

*(***SALLY*** just stares in utter awe at the idiocy of* **BELLE***.* **COOPER** *realizes they were teasing. He laughs and heads off –)*

SALLY. Don't go. Hey, if you're looking for a girl. We've got one right here. *(She offers up* **BELLE***.)*

COOPER. I'm flattered but –

SALLY. You don't want to pass this up son. This is the finest example of feminine pulchritude this side of the Mississippi. Yes sir...

(In rolls an old medicine wagon backdrop. SISTER LOVE'S HEART ELIXER.)

Song - ***GIRL OF YOUR DREAMS***

SALLY.

> STEP RIGHT UP AND GET AN EYEFUL OF THIS WARM
> AND TASTY TRIFLE
> GIRL LIKE THIS WILL MAKE YOUR PULSE RATE SOAR
>
> GOT A LOT OF CURVES AND EACH IS RIPE AS
> SUMMER GEORGIA PEACHES
> WHAT THE REBS WERE FIGHTING FOR
>
> FROM THE MANSION ANTEBELLUM SO SHE'S GOT
> NO CEREBELLUM
> SHE'S MUCH SWEETER THAN PRALINES

BELLE. Hey.

SALLY.

> YOU'LL THINK SOMEONE'S BEGUN BEGUINES FOR
> THE GIRL OF YOUR DREAMS
>
> *(****BELLE*** *glares at her, then switches tactics, offering* ***SALLY*** *up to* ***COOPER.****)*

BELLE.

> OR IT MAY BE SALLY
> YOU LONG FOR
> SHE'S LIKE THE JUNK THEY HAVE IN CHINA

SALLY. Hey.

BELLE.

> THAT'S A BOAT SO CLIMB ABOARD
> AND SHE'S A BARGAIN CAUSE SHE IS CHARGIN'
> HALF THE GOING RATE
> BUT KISS HER SQUARELY ON THE ANKLE
> THERE'S A WHOLE WORLD TO BE THANKFUL OF
> CAUSE BELIEVE ME PAL
> HEAVEN'S ABOVE

BOTH.

> STEP RIGHT UP RIGHT UP AND MEET THE GIRL OF
> YOUR DREAMS
> SHE'S GOT GOODIES IN HER POCKET
> TO FIRE UP YOUR ROCKET
> IF YOU KNOW WHAT I MEAN
> STEP RIGHT UP RIGHT UP AND MEET THE GIRL OF
> YOUR DREAMS

IF YOU WANT A DATE
YOU DON'T WANNA WAIT
COME AND MEET YOUR FATE
ONE TASTE AND YOU'LL SCREAM
FOR THE GIRL OF YOUR DREAMS.

(Both girls stare at each other and the kid gloves come off. They end up with dancing canes.)

SALLY.

PUT YOUR EAR UP NEXT TO BELLE'S AND YOU CAN
HEAR THE OCEAN SWELL
BUT I'VE YET TO SEE A MAN WHO MINDS OH NO.
THEY GLADLY PAY THE EXTRA DOLLAR CAUSE THE
CUFF MATCHES THE COLLAR
IT'S A LIE THAT LOVE IS BLIND

THINK OF THE PLEASURE SHE'LL PROVIDE AS LONG
AS YOU DON'T MIND PEROXIDE
NOT AS FAIR AS SHE MIGHT SEEM
BUT IF A DODO MAKES YOU GAGA SHE'S THE GIRL
OF YOUR DREAMS.

BELLE.	**SALLY.**
WHY NOT MAKE SALLY	DON'T PAY HER NO MIND
YOUR MIDNIGHT RIDE	I'M SURE YOU WILL FIND
SHE'S AS CUDDLY AS A BANK VAULT	
BUT NOT AS HARD TO GET INSIDE	SHE LEFT HERS BEHIND
SHE'S MEAN	NO I'M NOT
SHE POUTS	NO I DON'T
AND SHE'S SOFT AND WIDE	
IF YOU REALLY WANT TO SCHTOOP HER	
DRINK YOURSELF INTO A STUPOR NOW	
I'M TELLIN' YA PAL	
THAT'S THE ONLY WAY HOW	

(The canes become fencing swords. They end up whacking at each other.)

BOTH.

I TELL YA...STEP RIGHT UP RIGHT UP AND MEET THE
GIRL OF YOUR DREAMS
SHE'S GOT GOODIES IN THE LARDER
TO MAKE YOU LITTLE HARDER
IF YOU KNOW WHAT I MEAN
STEP RIGHT UP RIGHT UP AND MEET THE GIRL OF
YOUR DREAMS
IF YOU WANT A DAME

BELLE.

SHREW THAT YOU CAN TAME

SALLY.

IF YOU HAVE NO SHAME

BOTH.

YOU'LL PRIMP AND YOU'LL PREEN
FOR THE GIRL OF YOUR DREAMS.

(When the song ends they're each displaying the other for **COOPER***'s choosing. Trouble is, he's gone. Vanished.)*

SALLY. Oh no. Where'd he go?

(They go running upstairs in search of him. A moment later **DENISE** *comes out of the kitchen with* **COOPER** *on her heels.)*

COOPER. It's okay. You don't have to talk. I'll do it all. I got enough yak for both of us. I mean I can talk till the cows come home... *(Long pause, then to the audience...)* Now I didn't actually hear the cows come home, but evidently they had. I couldn't think of a thing to say. *(***DENISE*** scurries behind the bar and pours herself a hard shot of rye.)* Just when I was beginning to think she really didn't like me...

*(***DENISE*** pours two drinks. That's an invitation pal. So he looks to the audience and –)*

Excuse me.

(He leaps to the bar, drinks it. And when he puts the glass down, there's the book he lent her –)

COOPER. Did you finish this? Gosh, you're a fast reader. I read just a tad faster than mollassas. Course, I didn't learn how till I was twenty.

(They share a smile. Then **DENISE** *offers a second shot glass. She'll join him. Not a word between them. He pours two whiskeys.)*

COOPER. You like it?

(She shrugs and shakes her head.)

COOPER. Yeah. Kinda twisted. Deals a lot with death. *(She drinks.)* And cowards. *(He drinks.)* I have another one. Little happier fellah. You wanna try that? *(She nods, then gestures for a swap.)* What, you got one for me? Okay, you show me yours and I'll show you mine. *(Beat, then to the audience.)* I didn't mean that the way it sounded. Well maybe. Okay, I'll go get it.

(He vanishes upstairs. **DENISE** *stands for a moment, thinking, then she takes off for her own room just as* **GERT** *enters.)*

(She looks around then musters her courage and tip-toes over to the bar and risks a look to see if **MARTIN** *'s body is still there. Nothing there. She gets behind it for a better look and actually ducks down. Maybe he's under the shelves.)*

(She's still outta sight when **MARION** *comes in with a coil of rope.* **GERT** *pops up like a jack-in-the-box from behind the bar!)*

MARION. AHHHHH!

GERTIE. AHHHHHH!

GERTIE & MARION. AHHHHHH!

(Beat, while the two women stand statue-stiff like a duel at high noon.)

GERTIE. Where is he?

MARION. In the kitchen. Why didn't you say anything?

GERTIE. Guess I figured he finally got what he deserved. He was a despicable man.

MARION. He didn't try anything with you –

GERTIE. No. But I remember him from when my Daddy used to bring me… I mean…You know.

MARION. What are you going to do?

GERTIE. I'm not sure.

MARION. I'll tell you this Doll, if anyone found out it wouldn't look to good for – – some people.

GERTIE. So if I wanted to help – – some people – – I should just stay quiet.

MARION. If you could find it in your heart…

GERTIE. It's our secret. I give you my word. I won't tell a soul.

MARION. How old are you now Gert?

GERTIE. Twenty and a half.

MARION. I hated being twenty. Everytime you turn around somebody's trying to tell you what the hell – shoot! *(She flicks her own ear!)* Ow. Somebody's tellin' you what to do.

GERTIE. Yeah.

MARION. I was raised by my grandmother. Fire and brimstone.

GERTIE. Yeah.

MARION. Wanted me to be just like her. Like it wasn't even my life.

GERTIE. Exactly. That's it exactly.

MARION. So I ran away.

GERTIE. Really? Maybe that's it! Maybe I should –

MARION. I ended up here.

GERTIE. *(Stopped in her tracks. Heavy beat.)* Oh.

MARION. *(As if on cue, the wind kicks up and rattles the windows.)* Boy, that wind is really getting' loud.

HARD CORA. *(Entering from the bedrooms.)* Yup, and it'll get worse still. Until it's a ragin' deadly – aw to hell with it. Howdy Marion.

MARION. Cora.

HARD CORA. Can I buy you a drink?

MARION. *(***MARION** *and* **GERT** *lock eyes. Nod.)* Anytime Doll.

HARD CORA. That's if you don't mind drinkin' with a ranch hand like me.

MARION. I surely don't.

GERTIE. I don't either.

HARD CORA. *(Looking at her. For one moment these two connect.* **GERT** *has found her role model.)* Well then, set up a third. Cheers.

> *(While* **MARION** *starts to pour,* **CORA** *looks less sure of herself here, studying* **MARION**'s *hands.)*

HARD CORA. You sure got pretty hands, Marion.

MARION. Oh. Thanks.

HARD CORA. I can never seem to keep mine clean.

MARION. Soak 'em in lemon juice and vinegar.

HARD CORA. Don't ya just end up smellin' like a salad?

> *(Cheers. They drink.* **GERT** *nearly chokes on hers.* **CORA** *pats her on the back. Too hard, then way too daintily.* **CORA** *can't seem to find a balance.)*

GERTIE. What's it like to be a blacksmith?

HARD CORA. Hot. *(To* **MARION** *−)* What do you do about callouses?

GERTIE. Is it...I mean do you feel...is it exciting?

HARD CORA. No.

GERTIE. No? Not even a little?

HARD CORA. No.

GERTIE. It must be. Just a little.

HARD CORA. No. You work dawn till dust poundin' with a hammer, surrounded by fire and sweat. Actually, it's a lot like hell.

GERTIE. But it's better than being married.

HARD CORA. Definitely. *(***GERT** *looks hugely relieved. Everyone drinks again.* **CORA**'s *staring at her hands.)* But I don't want to be a blacksmith. What I really want is a ranch. Coupla thousand acres.

GERTIE. *(Totally inspired.)* Why don't you do it?

HARD CORA. Bank won't lend me that kind of money. Banker looks at me he don't see Rancher. Others look at me and don't see nothin' but. But I sure would like to see my own spread.

MARION. Nah, too much sun. My dreams are a dark hall with a single spotlight. Me in a red dress. Singin' to a crowd. Just for a moment, just one moment I can make them forget their blues. How 'bout you Gert?

GERTIE. Me? Nobody's ever asked... I don't have any...

HARD CORA. Everybody's got dreams.

GERTIE. No. Life is pretty black and white.

MARION. That's your momma talkin'.

HARD CORA. Go on now. Close your eyes. (**GERTIE** *does and Music kicks in, light and haunting.*) What do you see?

Song - *THE COLORS OF MY WORLD*

GERTIE.

THE MURKY BROWN HAZE BEHIND MY EYES
TURNS DARK AS TOMORROW UNFURLS
    THE TUNNEL'S END GLOW IS BLACK WITH
SHADOWS
THESE ARE THE COLORS OF MY WORLD

THE FAMED POT OF GOLD UNDER THE RAINBOW
WILL NEVER SHINE BRIGHT CAUSE THE SUN
DOESN'T SHOW
THERE'S NO SILVER LININGS IN MY CLOUDY DAYS
I LIVE IN A CAGE OF GREY

*(She stands there trembling. **CORA** and **MARION** exchange looks before...)*

MARION. Oh Darlin', there's color all around you. RED

HARD CORA.

YELLOW

BOTH.

GREEN PURPLE GOLD
FEEL YOUR RAINBOW

> FEEL YOUR RAINBOW
> FEEL YOUR RAINBOW

HARD CORA.

THE FIRE RED JOLT OF A GOOD SHOT OF RYE

MARION.

PINK BUBBLE BATHS MAKE YOUR TOES CURL

BOTH.

THE DEEP PURPLE HUSH OF SLEEPING PAST DAWN
THESE ARE THE COLORS OF MY WORLD

(The girls are getting chummy, embellishing on the other, adlibbing, "Oh, I got one," and "Oh baby that's a good one." It's a chick bond fest.)

MARION.

THE HOT CRIMSON BLUSH OF A GOOD LOVERS
TOUCH

HARD CORA.

HONEST SWEAT MAKES YOU SHINE LIKE A PEARL

GERTIE.

THE SOARING BLUE HIGH WHEN GIRLFRIENDS
CONFIDE

*(**GERT** stands to sing making **MARION** and **CORA**'s mouths drop in awe and delight.)*

GERTIE.

THESE ARE THE COLORS OF MY WORLD

ALL 3.

OF MY WORLD OF MY WORLD OF MY WORLD OH
YEAH MMMMMM OF MY WORLD

HARD CORA.

CHOCOLATE'S FIRST BITE IS A DUSKY BROWN KISS

GERTIE.

THERE'S PRIDE IN A BLUE DENIM GIRL

MARION.

THE SIMPLE WHITE JOY WHEN YOUR HAIRDO
BEHAVES

ALL 3.

THESE ARE THE COLORS OF MY WORLD

GERTIE & HARD CORA.

> RED YELLOW SILVER
> GREEN PURPLE AND GOLD
> THESE ARE THE COLORS
> OF MY WORLD
> BLUE AMBER VIOLET
> ORANGE CRIMSON
> COPPER
> THESE ARE THE COLORS
> OF MY WORLD

MARION.

> YOU'LL FIND IF YOU
> OPEN YOUR EYES
> THERE ARE COLORS IN
> YOUR WORLD
> THEY THRIVE &
> EXPLODE IN YOUR LIFE
>
> ALL THESE COLORS IN
> YOUR WORLD

ALL 3.

> THESE ARE THE COLORS

GERTIE. *(Timidly.)*

> THE COLORS

MARION & HARD CORA. Oh come on, Gert, you can do better than that. *(They pass her a bottle and she takes a swig.)*

> THESE ARE THE COLORS

GERTIE. *(She rips into the song, riffing like a rock diva.)*

> THE COLORS

MARION & HARD CORA. Whooo-hooooo.

ALL THREE.

> THESE ARE THE COLORS OF MY WORLD

(The song ends with deep felt closeness. The girls arms around each other. They're loose and a little tipsy from the hooch so MARION says playfully –)

MARION. Hey. I know what. Let's paint 'em.

HARD CORA. What?

MARION. Your nails.

HARD CORA. Paint 'em?.

MARION. We could do 'em up right now.

HARD CORA. Really? Nah.

MARION. Sure. I got some polish up in my room.

HARD CORA. Nah.

MARION. Some rouge too.

HARD CORA. Nah.

GERTIE. Why not?

HARD CORA. Okay.

(So **CORA** *and* **GERT** *down another shot for courage and head upstairs.* **GERT** *pauses long enough to grab the bottle of hooch and take it with her. Just as they head up the stairs,* **BELLE** *and* **SALLY** *are coming back down.* **MARION** *hesitates.)*

MARION. You two go on up, I'll be right behind ya.

SALLY. Storm's getting bad. If we're gonna do this we better do it now.

MARION. Come on.

(They fade into the kitchen. We hear some grunts and groans from out there, then they reappear, dragging **MARTIN.** *They don't get far when –)*

COOPER. Sorry I took so long. I think someone's been through my saddlebags –

(He freezes as he sees the body. What happens next is a whirlwind, the girls searching for some clue how to play this. They're improvising like mad.)

COOPER. Dear God.

(The girls look at **COOPER**, *then to the body they carry.)*

MARION/SALLY/BELLE. AHHH!

(They drop the body as if they've never seen it before. How'd that get here?!)

COOPER. What happened?!

MARION. I don't know.

COOPER. Who is he?

MARION. I don't... ah...

BELLE. Martin!

COOPER. The bartender?

BELLE. Yeah.

COOPER. He's shot!

MARION. Really?

COOPER. Where'd you find him?

MARION. In the – behind the – over the – under the – by the – *(She points.)*

COOPER. Where's my gun?

MARION. What do you need a gun for?

COOPER. Did you see anyone else?

MARION. What do you need a gun for?!

COOPER. Was there anyone else out there?

BELLE. I didn't see anyone.

COOPER. The blood's dry. This coulda happened hours ago. How is it you didn't find him till now?

SALLY. *(Oh no. She's moved to the center of the room.)* Marshall?

COOPER. What?!

(The room freezes for half a beat. The three girls lock eyes. Well, that answers that question. Now what?)

COOPER. *(To the audience.)* Ever have one of those moments you just wish you could do again. Just go back in time and put the cat back in the bag?

SALLY. Are you really a Marshall?

COOPER. Yeah.

SALLY. Oh, Marshall. Is he really dead?

COOPER. Yeah.

SALLY. *(Doing a bad* **BELLE** *imitation.)* Oh no. Oh no, oh no.

COOPER. Take it easy.

SALLY. Who did it?

COOPER. I don't know.

SALLY. What if they're still here? What if –

COOPER. *(Right up to her, hands on her shoulders.)* Easy. I don't think they're still here. They woulda showed themselves by now.

SALLY. Marshall?

COOPER. Yeah?

SALLY. I'm really sorry.

(She knees him, driving his nuts far north. **COOP***'s breath is sucked away as he crumbles. He looks to the audience.)*

COOPER. Okay, I can't tell you how much that hurt. Almost as much as – *(SMASH!* **SALLY***'s grabbed a bottle off the bar and shatters it on the back of his head. He goes down like a bull. Tableau for a second as the three women survey what just happened.)*

BELLE. Oh no.

MARION. Alright, what happens now?

SALLY. I don't know.

BELLE. Oh no.

MARION. How can you not know? I thought you were in charge.

SALLY. When did I get to be in charge. You said you ran this place.

BELLE. Oh no.

MARION. You hit him with the bottle.

SALLY. You said Martin's "M" was your's.

BELLE. Oh no.

MARION. Well, this is great. We got him all laid out. Now what do we do?

SALLY. Kill him?

BELLE. Oh NO!!

SALLY. Think! He's a Marshal. If he comes too he'll arrest us as accessories to murder. They wouldn't think twice about hangin' a bunch of whores. Now come on.

BELLE. No. I won't do it.

SALLY. We just stick him outside with Martin. No one'll even know. No body, no crime.

BELLE. I can't.

SALLY. *(Playing her trump card)* What about Westley?

BELLE. What?

SALLY. What if he comes back and you're a convicted felon.

MARION. Sal –

SALLY. You've waited so long to be Missus Beufort Westley Barker. You gonna let this man keep you from that?

BELLE. I can't –

SALLY. Well, I sure as ain't gonna hang. *(She tugs out a knife, sweeping in on the defenseless* **COOPER**, *raises it, and –)*

DENISE. NOOOOO!

(She's standing in the doorway, a huge book in her hand – one she's meant to share with **COOPER**. *She drops it and as she rushes in, putting herself between* **SAL** *and* **COOP**.)

SALLY. Guess I wasn't clear about the whole not talking thing.

DENISE. *(Throwing herself over* **COOPER**, *protecting him.)* NO!!

(Her voice shocks everyone into silence. **SAL** *lowers the knife.)*

BELLE. So what now?

SALLY. Now we got –

HARD CORA. *(Offstage.)* YEEHAW!

(CORA and GERT can be heard braying drunken laughter from upstairs. Oh no! **BELLE** *and* **SALLY** *scramble to get* **MARTIN** *hidden. They do a lousy job.* **DENISE** *and* **MARION** *wrestle* **COOPER** *into a chair,* **DENISE** *curling in his lap to make it look like he's still wide awake and functioning.)*

(CORA and GERT explode into the room and oh-no, they are drunk out of their minds. **GERT**'s *draining the last drops from a bottle. She's dressed exactly like* **CORA** *was.* **CORA** *on the other extreme, has obviously raided* **MARION**'s *closet. She is decked out in a dress, petticoats, boas, hair swept up, nails done.)*

HARD CORA. Hey everybody. *(CORA does a little turn like a drunken model on a fashion runway. Music kicks in.)*

BELLE. Cora? .

SALLY. Wow, look at you.

GERTIE. Isn't she the greatest?

MARION. What's gotten into you two?

Song - *JUST ONE OF THE GIRLS*

HARD CORA.

I'M TRYING TO UNRAVEL THIS MYSTERY
THE MIRROR IS WITHHOLDING THE
REFLECTION OF ME
WHO I AM AND WHAT YOU SEE JUST DON'T
COINCIDE
THE WOMAN PEOPLE SEE AIN'T THE WOMAN
INSIDE
GONNA CHANGE MY IMAGE GONNA SET THE
RECORD STRAIGHT
THERE'S SOME CATCHIN' UP TO DO AND I'M
CHARGIN' FROM THE GATE
I SAID–
WHAM-BAM, HERE I AM, ONE OF THE GIRLS
I SAID WHAM, HERE I AM, ONE OF THE GIRLS
RIGHT HERE, RIGHT NOW, I'M CHANGING MY WORLD
STAND BACK DARLIN' I'M JUST ONE OF THE GIRLS

(She takes a closer look at **COOPER**. *Huh? So to cover,* **DENISE** *waves his hand for him. 'HI'.)*

GERTIE.

I'M TIRED OF BECOMING WHAT'S EXPECTED OF ME
HIDING IN A SKIN OF FEM-IN-NIN-ITY
THERE'S A WOLF BURIED INSIDE THESE SHEEP-SKIN
CLOTHES
AND WHO SHE IS OR WHAT SHE WANTS NOBODY
KNOWS
TRAPPED WITHIN A GILDED CAGE DYING TO BE FREE
WELL I CUT THAT SUCKER LOOSE AND BABY
WHISKEY WAS THE KEY

(Through this number, **CORA** *and* **GERT** *are vamping for the world to see.* **MARTIN** *'s body starts to topple out of hiding. Ahhh! So to cover,* **MARION** *snags the girls attention by joining the song and keeping them focused downstage.* **BELLE** *and* **SALLY** *try to cover by catching* **MARTIN** *and dancing with him.* **DENISE** *is forced to do the same with the unconscious* **COOPER** *so no one notices Martin. So here we are with two drunk women dancing with a dead-man chorus.)*

GERTIE.

WHAM-BAM, HERE I AM, ONE OF THE GIRLS

MARION, GERTIE, AND HARD CORA.

I SAID WHAM, HERE I AM, ONE OF THE GIRLS

RIGHT HERE, RIGHT NOW, I'M CHANGING MY WORLD

STAND BACK DARLIN' I'M JUST ONE OF THE GIRLS

HARD CORA.

FOUND A NEW OBSESSION

TO CHANGE THE WORLD'S IMPRESSION

SHOW MY PETITE AND DAMSEL-ISH SIDE

GERTIE.

PEOPLE CAN EXPECT'LL

LOT FROM MRS. JECKYL

'CAUSE NOW I'VE GOT NOTHING TO HIDE OOOOH

HARD CORA, GERTIE.	**MARION, SALLY AND BELLE**
WHAM-	WHAM
BAM,	BAM
HERE I AM,	HERE I AM
ONE OF THE GIRLS	
I SAID WHAM,	WHAM
HERE I AM,	HERE I AM
ONE OF THE GIRLS	
RIGHT HERE,	RIGHT HERE
RIGHT NOW,	RIGHT NOW
I'M CHANGING MY WORLD	CHANGIN' MY WORLD
STAND BACK DARLIN'	STAND BACK, STAND BACK

ALL THE GIRLS.

I'M JUST ONE OF THE GIRLS

*(Music ends. **CORA** strikes a pose as **GERT** promptly passes out. THUNK! **CORA** looks at her, then passes out too. **DENISE** can't hold **COOPER** so he slithers to the floor. And the girls can let go of **MARTIN**, so he hits like a bag of cement. **SALLY, BELLE, MARION** and **DENISE** look around at the body strewn floor as the music buttons out. BLACKOUT)*

End of Act One

ACT II

Scene 1

(Everyone is right where we left them. Music sneaks up and **COOPER** *sits up and sings to the audience again.)*

Song - ONE OF THOSE DAYS

COOPER.

MY SECRET WAS OUT AND THE PLOT JUST GOT
THICKER
NO BODY KNEW WHAT THE TALE HELD IN STORE
BUT BETWEEN THE FRYING PANS, BOTTLES AND
LIQUOR
I SPENT AN AWFUL LOT OF TIME ON THE FLOOR
Yodel-lei-eee.

HAVE YOU EVER HAD ONE OF THOSE DAYS
YOU KNOW THE KIND WHERE YOU CAN'T SEEM TO
WIN
GET ALONG LITTLE DOGGIES IT'S ONE OF THOSE
DAYS

GERTIE & HARD CORA. *(Sitting up and singing to the audience.)*

LEAST YOU'RE NOT DRUNK WITH THREE SHEETS IN
THE WIND
SUN UP THIS MORNING AND THINGS WERE JUST
DANDY

GERTIE.

MY MOTHER GOT TALKING WE STARTED TO DOUBT

GERTIE & HARD CORA.

WE DROWN OUR SORROWS IN A WHISKEY BOTTLE
OUR SORROWS COULD SWIM BUT WE JUST PASSED
OUT.

GERTIE. <hic>   **CORA.** <Ptooie>

51

GERTIE, HARD CORA, AND COOPER.

HAVE YOU EVER HAD JUST ONE OF THOSE DAYS
YOUR BACK'S AT THE WALL AND THERE'S NO PLACE
TO HIDE
YIPPIKAIYEA IT'S ONE OF THOSE DAYS

MARION, BELLE, SALLY, AND DENISE. (*Standing and taking the stage.*)

LEAST YOU'RE NOT WANTED FOR A HOMICIDE

MARION.	**SALLY.**	**BELLE.**
Ow.	Ha!	GAWD

WE WERE JUST MINDIN' OUR OWN HUMBLE
BUSINESS
WHEN MARTIN CAME BACK AND SHATTERED OUR
HOPE
THINGS GOT OUTTA HAND AND A GUN IT GOT IN
ONE
MAY SEE TOMORROW FROM THE END OF A ROPE

(*And the song takes a strange little turnm the cast now stands across the front of the strage. Each of their little guttural sounds become a chorus of worry. And the song's getting faster, and faster, and faster…*)

YO-HIC-PTOO-OW-HA-GAWD YO-HIC-PTOO-OW-HA-
GAWD
YO-HIC-PTOO-OW-HA-GAWD YO-HIC-PTOO-OW-HA-
GAWD
YO-HIC-PTOO-OW-HA-GAWD YO-HIC-PTOO-OW-HA-
GAWD

ALL.

HAVE YOU EVER HAD ONE OF THOSE DAYS
YOU ASKED FOR APPLES GOT ORANGES INSTEAD
YIPPEE AND YEEHAW IT'S ONE OF THOSE DAYS

MARTIN.

AW QUITCHER BITCHIN' AT LEAST YOU AIN'T DEAD

(*He falls back down, one rigor mortised arm sticking up. Now the song is getting out of control.*)

ALL.

HAVE YOU EVER HAD ONE OF THOSE DAYS
STUCK 'TWEEN A HARD PLACE AND A ROCK
GIDDYUP COWBOY IT'S ONE OF THOSE DAYS

MARTIN.

TIME TO STOP WHINNIN' GET BACK TO THE PLOT

ALL.

IT'S ONE OF THOSE DAYS. IT'S ONE OF THOSE DAYS. IT'S ONE OF THOSE DAYS.

(Everyone runs madly for their places, barely making it before Music out. Those that should be passed out, pass out. Those that should be in shock, get shocked. It's only a few minutes later. **COOP** *is starting to come around.* **DENISE** *is cradling him,* **BELLE,** **SAL** *and* **MARION** *hover around, guilty as heck. Ahhhhhhhh... ..)*

DENISE. *(Only to* **COOPER***)* Shhhh. It's okay. Shhhh.

MARION. Denise. You're aware he's A MARSHALL!

DENISE. Shhh. We're together now.

SALLY. That can't be a good career move.

COOPER. *(Sitting up, rubbing his head.)* How'd you know I was a Marshall?

BELLE. Sally went through your stuff.

SALLY. Read the forehead. I really need a tattoo.

COOPER. What else do you know about me?

MARION. More? There's more to know?

SALLY. Ain't you just a bundle of secrets.

COOPER. It was you that went through my room?

BELLE. That's not really your room. It's Martin's.

COOPER. So. That M stands for Martin's place, not Marion's place.

MARION. No.

BELLE. Yes.

MARION. Yes.

COOPER. So who killed him?

(Beat.)

SALLY. I did.

MARION. I did.

BELLE. Me.

COOPER. Come on ladies. He was only shot twice. At the outside it could only have been two of you. Now what happened?

(And they go into a story, each embellishing on the other.)

MARION. Well, he was supposed to be driving cattle with the other men.

SALLY. But he snuck back.

MARION. And he came upstairs.

SAL & BELLE. To my room! –

MARION. Which is right next to mine.

BELLE. And he broke down the door.

SALLY. He was drunk.

MARION. Shoutin' and singin'.

BELLE. He was a lousy singer.

MARION. And then he stormed to the bed –

SALLY. Yanked me to my feet, and I –

DENISE. – hid behind the closet door. Hopin' he'd go away, but he wouldn't. He caught me, threw me down. Then he pulled out that big knife he carries all the time. And when he started…I reached up and the gun was just there. I didn't even hear it go off.

COOPER. It was you? It was her?

(The way the other girls look away is his answer. Not the answer he wanted.)

DENISE. I wasn't even sure he was dead. He could have just been asleep. But then he didn't move. And he didn't move.

MARION. That sounds like Martin.

COOPER. *(To the audience.)* This ever happen to you? You finally find your destiny, your soul mate, your reason to live. She's a killer.

MARION. So what happens now?

COOPER. I don't know.

MARION. You don't know?

COOPER. No.

SALLY. You must know.

COOPER. Sorry. I don't.

SALLY. How can you not know? How can he not know?

COOPER. I'm caught horseless in the middle of the worst dust storm in a decade. Trapped inside a saloon with several ladies from town and a dead body.

BELLE. What do you normally do in a situation like this?

COOPER. I… I ah… *(To the audience)* I truly didn't have an answer for that.

DENISE. Are you gonna arrest me?

COOPER. I'm not sure.

DENISE. Why not? I shot him.

COOPER. I realize that. We should just turn this over to the local sheriff.

DENISE. He and Martin were best friends.

COOPER. Well I'm outta ideas. Let's forget the whole thing.

MARION. Gee, this is an interestin' turn.

SALLY. Yeah, this is not what I expected at all.

(Just then **CORA** *starts to moan. She's comin' round.)*

BELLE. Oh no.

SALLY. What about him?

MARION. What about them?

COOPER. I vote we don't panic 'em. All those in favor?

MARION, BELLE & SALLY. Aye.

(And **COOPER** *hoists* **MARTIN** *to his feet, readying to potato-sack him over his shoulder.)*

DENISE. Why are you doin' this?

COOPER. We just hit the trouble jackpot, we don't need to share the wealth. Open the door.

BELLE. *(Doing it.)* That's just what we were going to do.

(So he drags **MARTIN** *out into the storm. Once he's gone, they slam the door against the raging dust and* **CORA** *sits up rubbing her head.)*

HARD CORA. Ooooooohhh.

MARION. *(To* **SALLY***.)* This is like a nightmare.

SALLY. Ever have the one where you go to work in your underwear? *(They both look down. They're standing there in their underwear. Oops.* **CORA** *tries to get to her feet. Only manages to roll around on the floor Curly style.)*

BELLE. Wow, Cora are you alright?

HARD CORA. Right as rain. I have just temporarily relinquished control of the left side of my body. And sacrificed any sense of direction. I'm standing up, right?

MARION. Yeah. *(***MARION** *pulls* **CORA** *to her feet.)*

HARD CORA. Well hell, I'm top of the world then. Ha. Looks like Gert can't hold her whishkey. *(She helps* **GERT** *to her feet so the two drunken women are just standin' in each other's arms.* **CORA** *looks deep into* **GERT***'s eyes.)* Damn. She's purty, ain't she? Gert. Gertie. *(She strokes some hair out of* **GERT***'s face.)*

GERTIE. Hiii iiii iiiiii.

HARD CORA. Howdy.

GERTIE. Cora. Did we have lunch?

HARD CORA. Nope. Reckon we skipped it.

GERTIE. Too bad. That means this must be breakfast.

> *(***GERT***'s about to throw up. Oh no, the girls hover around.* **CORA** *chucks her over her shoulder fireman style. They rush out,* **BELLE** *holding the spittoon for good use. They all vanish into the kitchen, leaving* **DENISE** *alone in the room, staring at the front door. In fact, she hasn't moved since* **COOPER** *went out. Two seconds later he comes pounding back in, the wind nearly ripping the door off. He hacks and coughs. He's truly afraid now.)*

COOPER. *(Coughing dust to the audience –)* I didn't think it could get that bad.

DENISE. *(This is a life changing moment for her.)* Why would you do that?

COOPER. What?

DENISE. You just made yourself an accessory. Why? No man's ever done anything like that for me.

COOPER. 'Bout time they did.

DENISE. Why?

COOPER. Cause you deserve it. Sheriff shoulda stopped him.

DENISE. But I'm just a… I'm a… You know what I am.

COOPER. Yes. I do. And nobody should be treated that way.

DENISE. Are you real?

COOPER. I could be real if you'll let me.

DENISE. But I'm not worthy of a hero.

COOPER. I'm not a hero. Please, don't make me that.

DENISE. It's all right. I know all about heroes.

Song - STORYBOOK ROMANCE

SPENT LIFE BETWEEN PAGES OF STORY-BOOK ROMANCE
   WAITING THROUGH BEST OF TIMES AND WORST TIMES
      FOR MY CHANCE
A KNIGHT TO COME AND SAVE ME
A SHINING PALADIN
   TO CLOSE A CHAPTER AND LET ONE BEGIN
   ONCE UPON A TIME, I BELIEVED IN FAIRY TALES
      KNIGHTS ARE ALWAYS WHITE
      BUT THAT'S NOT TRUE
I SEE YOU STANDING HERE THEN READ THE PAGES OF MY HEART
      AND WONDER STILL
      COULD IT BE YOU

BOOKS WERE THE ONLY ESCAPE
FROM THE HELL MY LIFE HAD BEEN
   NEVERMORE WAS I THE ANGELIC HEROINE
A DOVE TOO SOILED TO FLY NOW
I GOT WHAT I DESERVED
   THIS TELL-TALE HEART WOULD NEVER FIND LOVE THEN

THERE YOU WERE
  ONCE UPON A TIME, I BELIEVED IN FAIRY TALES
   ANGELS HAD THEIR WINGS
   AND DREAMS COME TRUE
  CAST THE BOOKS ASIDE THE ONLY THING THAT
THEY GOT RIGHT
   WAS THE HOPE IN MY SOUL
   THAT IT BE YOU

COOPER.	DENISE.
I'M NO ANGEL	I'M NO PRINCESS IN A TOWER

COOPER.	DENISE.
I'M NO SAVIOR	I DON'T EARN DULCINEA'S LOVE

COOPER.	DENISE.
I'M NO HERO	THE BLACKEST WINGS CAN GLEAM AGAIN

  TO SOAR THE SKIES ABOVE

DENISE.
ONCE UPON A TIME
 COOPER.
 CAN I BE WHAT YOU WANT
  DENISE.
  I BELIEVED IN FAIRY TALES
   COOPER.
   CAN I BE WHAT YOU NEED

DENISE.
ANGELS HAD THEIR WINGS
 COOPER.
 CAN I MAKE YOUR

TOGETHER.
DREAMS COME TRUE

DENISE.
CAST THE BOOKS ASIDE
 COOPER.
 SEE MYSELF IN YOUR EYES
  DENISE.
  DON'T COMPARE TO MY LIFE

COOPER.

A MAN I DON'T RECOGNIZE

DENISE.

CAN MY SOUL FLY

TOGETHER.

SINCE I MET YOU – SINCE I MET YOU

(Song ends and just as they are about to kiss we –)

(FADE TO BLACK)

Scene 2

(The lights come up along with the wind. The poker table is still down front, but the bar has vanished. Now there are two doors lining the upstage wall. These are the rooms upstairs. We'll fade between upstairs and downstairs. Lights will do most of the work, but the stairs will help. When we're downstairs, the stairs are visible. They retract when we go upstairs. Right now, COOPER is upstairs talkin' to the audience again.)

COOPER. So this is what love feels like. For the first time in forever my future actually looked bright. *(He turns to walk into the room when the wind gets louder. Oh yeah–)* Except for the whole raging dust storm thing. *(Louder wind)* That was getting progressively worse *(Louder. COOPER talks to the sound guy.)* And threatening to collapse this entire building down on top of us, we get it. *(Back to audience)* Now Denise and I were in my room – we were upstairs here – just – Um – DOWNSTAIRS. Now that's where some interesting things were happening. Downstairs.

(The lights come up on the "downstairs." SALLY and BELLE are playing poker.)

SALLY. Three deuces.

BELLE. What do you call it again when you got all one color?

SALLY. Crap. They all have to be the same suit. That'd be a flush.

BELLE. Like if they were all diamonds, or the little hearts.

SALLY. Yeah. They all have to be the same little whatever.

*(***MRS. LOUISE STYLES** *comes in lugging her quilt and looking frantically for –)*

LOUISE STYLES. Gertrude? Gertrude? Where is she? Have you seen my daughter?

SALLY. No. *(**LOUISE** starts to walk away.)*

BELLE. Mrs. Styles?! There's something I think you should know. *(**LOUISE** stops.)* Does a flush beat three deuces?

LOUISE STYLES. What? I don't – Yes – ach – Gertrude.

BELLE. Flush. I like this game. *(She reels in her winnings.)*

(Disgruntled, **LOUISE STYLES** *heads upstairs. The stairs hide and the lights shift to "upstairs." We can see* **MARION** *tending to a passed out* **CORA** *and* **GERT** *in* **CORA***'s room.* **DENISE** *and* **COOPER** *are together in his room cuddling.)*

COOPER. Best beginning ever?

DENISE. Charles Dickens. It was the best of times –

COOPER. We're in the middle of a dust storm. It was the worst of times.

DENISE. Nevermore.

COOPER. *(Into her eyes.)* Nevermore. Okay, favorite book.

DENISE. Mansfield Park. Jane Austen. Read it twice.

COOPER. Don't know it.

DENISE. Oh. It's about this poor girl who finds true love in spite of her social standing. Yours?

COOPER. Victor Hugo. Les Miserables.

DENISE. Isn't the lawman in that book the bad guy?

COOPER. It's a very real story.

DENISE. Had you pegged for a hero.

COOPER. No. The hero was Fontene. She gave up everything for her daughter. In the end became a prostitute to pay for her –

DENISE. Her father's medicine?

COOPER. No. Her daughter's.

DENISE. Right. Must be confusing it with a similar story.

COOPER. One you're familiar with?

DENISE. Oh yeah. Nearly autobiographical. Best ending?

COOPER AND DENISE. Happily ever after... *(She sits in his lap.)*

LOUISE STYLES. *(Banging on his door.)* Mr. Cooper. Have you seen my daughter?

COOPER. *(Rocketing to his feet, dumping* **DENISE** *on the floor.)* No ma'am.

(LOUISE turns to leave and catches sight of GERT's scarf hanging on his door knob. She bangs again.)

LOUISE STYLES. Then perhaps you can tell me why Gert's scarf is hanging on your knob?

COOPER. Excuse me?

LOUISE STYLES. *(Rattling the knob.)* I'd better check for myself.

COOPER. *(As DENISE rises for the door.)* What are you doing?

DENISE. She wants to check your knob.

COOPER. Tell her it's fine. Don't open.

DENISE. Why not?

COOPER. You, me, in a room. I don't want her judging you.

DENISE. I'm not afraid.

COOPER. I don't want her judging me.

LOUISE STYLES. Who are you talking to?

COOPER. Nobody.

LOUISE STYLES. Yourself or another nobody? Open this door.

(Just then MARION comes out of GERT and CORA's room. LOUISE corners her, pointing to COOPER's room.)

LOUISE STYLES. I demand you open that room.

MARION. I can't do that.

LOUISE STYLES. I think he may have my Gertrude in there.

MARION. Cooper? No. A white knight would never tarnish his sword and armor that way. Would he?

LOUISE STYLES. *(Mollified.)* No. I suppose you're right. But where is she? Good heavens, you don't suppose she's with the expectorant queen, do you?

(She moves for CORA's door. MARION throws herself in front of the doorjamb like a barricade.)

MARION. You can't go in there. Maybe she's in your room?

LOUISE STYLES. I looked.

MARION. Well she's a little thing. Check under the bed.

LOUISE STYLES. I did.

MARION. Well ain't you thorough. *(***LOUISE** *tries to bully past so* **MARION** *shifts gears.)* You know, we don't really know anything about Cooper do we? Maybe he's got her in there right now.

LOUISE STYLES. Good heavens.

*(***MARION** *rushes to the door and barely even touches the knob.)*

MARION. Locked. Bolted. Unbreakable without a key. It's downstairs on mmmmbeel, grummmpbllе blah. Hurry.

(So **LOUISE** *starts downstairs. When she's gone* **MARION** *bangs on* **COOPER***'s door –)*

MARION. She's coming back!

(Lights fade upstairs and come up downstairs just as **LOUISE** *enters down the staircase.* **SALLY***'s dealt cards and* **BELLE** *picks them up one at a time, and with each card she looks at she lets out an increasing squeal of delight.)*

SALLY. Is that your poker face?

BELLE. Shush, I'm thinkin'.

SALLY. Well maybe I should come back in a week or so.

LOUISE STYLES. Where do you people keep the room keys?

BELLE. We don't use room keys. *(Wink.* **LOUISE** *moans in worry and heads up the stairs again as –)*

SALLY. Ten Dollars

BELLE. Match.

SALLY. You say call.

BELLE. Call.

SALLY. Three deuces.

BELLE. Seven eight nine ten prince.

SALLY. A straight?! Son of a bitch.

BELLE. *(Raking in her loot.)* Did I win? I like this game.

(Lights and stairs cross fade to upstairs. **MARION** *has gotten* **GERT** *out of* **CORA***'s room.)*

MARION. Gert. Come on, wake up. What would your momma say?

GERTIE. Eleven stitches to the inch.

> *(**MARION** turns **GERT** away from her mom as **LOUISE**
> enters. **GERT** keeps popping up but **MARION** keeps
> hiding **GERT**'s head. **LOUISE** can only see **GERT** from
> behind, but since she's dressed in **CORA**'s clothes, guess
> who **LOUISE** thinks it is…)*

LOUISE STYLES. They said they don't use keys –

GERTIE. Find a man Gertrude –

LOUISE STYLES. Look at this.

GERTIE. Learn to cook Gertrude.

LOUISE STYLES. What a disgrace..

MARION. *(Thinking **LOUISE** knows it's **GERT** –)* Don't be too
hard on her. She's just drunk. It wasn't her fault.

LOUISE STYLES. I don't know why you insist on covering for
that… Blacksmith.

MARION. Cora? Cora. Right. This is Cora.

LOUISE STYLES. Comes from a lack of proper upbringing.
If she had a mother who knew how to raise a daughter.
I'd like to have a word with you.

> *(Just then **COOPER** and **DENISE** come out of their room,
> unseen by **LOUISE**. **MARION** uses them as distraction.)*

MARION. Is that Cooper over there?

> *(So now **LOUISE** heads to **COOPER**. **MARION** tries
> to dump **GERT** back in **CORA**'s room. But the door is
> locked. She fumbles for a moment then is forced to dump
> **GERT** like a load of bricks into **COOPER**'s room. She
> shuts the door.)*

LOUISE STYLES. Mister Cooper. You're hiding something.

COOPER. *(Freezing in his tracks.)* Who told you? What have
you heard?

LOUISE STYLES. About what?

COOPER. …nothing.

LOUISE STYLES. Nothing.

COOPER. Fine by me. *(He turns to leave again.)*

LOUISE STYLES. I demand to know where my daughter is.

COOPER. No idea.

LOUISE STYLES. I heard voices in your room –

DENISE. It's alright Missus Styles. It wasn't Gert, it was –

COOPER. Nobody.

LOUISE STYLES. Lot of them going around. You won't mind if I check.

COOPER. Swell. *(They go marching back to the door.)* See for yourself.

MARION. NO!

COOPER. I got nothing to hide. *(He swings open the door and sees GERT on the floor. He swings back and covers –)* Except laundry. It's a mess. The fringe is all tangled. I'm so embarrassed, really –

LOUISE STYLES. I saw something. That was Cora –

HARD CORA. *(Coming out of her room still in the dress and boa.)* Hey everybody. What about me?

LOUISE STYLES. *(Looking at the dress. Two seconds ago wasn't she in pants?)* What happened to you?

HARD CORA. Got feminated.

GERTIE. *(Popping out of COOPER's room.)* Isn't she the greatest?

LOUISE STYLES. Gertrude! What are you doing in a man's room?

GERTIE. I wasn't.

LOUISE STYLES. Don't lie.

HARD CORA. She ain't missus Styles. She was in here with me!

MARION. Not helping. Not helping.

LOUISE STYLES. *(Pissed again.)* Come along Gertrude. I don't want you catching callouses.

GERTIE. Mother, there's no reason to be rude.

LOUISE STYLES. Manners are for people on the same level of the food chain dear.

GERTIE. Why do you have to be – why do you – Maybe we could learn something.

LOUISE STYLES. When I want you to learn to break wind or spit your name in the snow, I'll send you to that woman. In the mean time, I'll teach you all you need to know.

(And everybody starts heading downstairs. The lights come up on **BELLE** *and* **SALLY** *still at the poker table. Now the doors vanish from upstairs, the bar rolls in and we're back downstairs for the rest of the scene.)*

SALLY. Full house.

BELLE. Four A's. I don't see why this game is so hard. Westley should've had me play. Whose deal?

SALLY. We're not playin' that no more. We're playin' gin, dollar a point.

BELLE. Like gin rummy?

SALLY. Dollar a point. Deal.

(More wind. Louder. **LOUISE** *and the others come in. She sits* **GERT** *in a chair near the bar and jams the quilt in her hands. She sits next to her daughter and picks up the needle. The wind gets louder. Scarier.* **COOPER** *is the last one down the stairs and he heads right to the audience.)*

COOPER. So you could see how things were pretty much under control. Just another boring day. That is, until the storm got worse. *(There's a HUGE CRASH. The others look nervously at the building, wondering if it's gonna bury them.)* Course, we didn't know just how bad it was gonna get.

(Suddenly there's another loud CRASH and the wind rages. **BELLE** *and* **SALLY** *run to* **MARION** *like kids wanting to climb into momma's bed during a thunderstorm.)*

DENISE. What was that?

MARION. That ain't nothin'.

BELLE. Sounded like something.

MARION. It's just noise. *(Another HUGE CRASH from outside.)*

SALLY. What if it ain't? What if –

MARION. Just noise. Hell, we can be louder than that. Come on. We can be louder...

Song - DANCE WITH THE DEVIL

MARION.

CLAP YOUR HANDS AND GET TO STOMPIN'
ON YOUR FEET LET'S MAKE SOME NOISE
MOTHER NATURE'S BANSHEE BAWLIN'
SCREAM RIGHT BACK LET'S HEAR YOUR VOICE
REBEL, RAISE HELL, REPEL THE THINGS THAT SCARE
YOU
    NO TEARS, YOUR FEARS, DISAPPEAR IF YOU DARE
TO
PARTY IN THE FACE OF DANGER,
HOWL AT THE MOON IF THERE AIN'T SUNLIGHT
DON'T GIVE OUT AND DON'T GIVE IN AND
DON'T GO QUIET INTO THAT GOOD NIGHT
LAUGH SING, SHOUT SCREAM,
BLOW STEAM OFF THIS HEARTACHE
SING LOUD, STAND PROUD
SOMEHOW DAY WILL BREAK
IN DIRE CIRCUMSTANCE, YOU GOTTA DANCE AND
FACE THE FRAY
IF NERO FIDDLED LOUDER THEN ROME WOULD
STAND TODAY

GERTIE.

TODAY

HARD CORA.

TODAY

MARION, GERTIE AND HARD CORA.

DANCE WITH THE DEVIL WHEN HELL COMES A
CALLIN'
WHISTLE IN THE DARK WHEN MIDNIGHT ROLLS
AROUND
YOU GOTTA SING LIKE AN ANGEL ON THE EVE OF
DESTRUCTION
WHEN NIGHTMARES KNOCK ON YOUR DOOR

JUST STAND YOUR GROUND
AND DON'T BACK DOWN
MAKE A JOYFUL SOUND
AND DON'T BACK DOWN
JUST STAND YOUR GROUND

MARION.

STEEL YOUR NERVES AND BITE THE BULLET
ROSEN UP YOUR SPINE A BIT
THE REAPER AIN'T SO GRIM WHEN LAUGHIN'
DANCE UNTIL YOUR SIDES'LL SPLIT
LAUGH SING, SHOUT SCREAM,
BLOW STEAM OFF THIS HEARTACHE
SING LOUD, STAND PROUD
SOMEHOW DAY WILL BREAK
WHEN JUDGMENT DAY ARRIVES LET LOOSE WITH A
BATTLE CRY
IF THEY'D DANCED WHEN THE FLOOD BEGAN
ATLANTIS WOULD BE DRY

CORA/GERTIE.   REST OF CAST.

DRY DRY   DRY-DRY-DRY-DRY

ALL

DANCE WITH THE DEVIL WHEN HELL COMES A
CALLIN'
WHISTLE IN THE DARK WHEN MIDNIGHT ROLLS
AROUND
YOU GOTTA SING LIKE AN ANGEL ON THE EVE OF
DESTRUCTION
WHEN NIGHTMARES KNOCK ON YOUR DOOR
JUST STAND YOUR GROUND
AND DON'T BACK DOWN
MAKE A JOYFUL SOUND
AND DON'T BACK DOWN
JUST STAND YOUR GROUND

(* *Dance break* * *)*

REST OF CAST.	MARION
AAAAAHHHH DANCE WITH THE DEVIL	DANCE WITH THE DEVIL
WHEN HELL COMES A CALLIN'	HELL COMES A CALLIN'
WHISTLE IN THE DARK	
WHEN MIDNIGHT ROLLS AROUND	MIDNIGHT ROLLS AROUND
SING LIKE AN ANGEL	
ON THE EVE OF DESTRUCTION	
WHEN NIGHTMARES KNOCK ON YOUR DOOR	
JUST STAND YOUR GROUND	STAND YOUR GROUND
AND DON'T BACK DOWN	DON'T BACK DOWN
MAKE A JOYFUL SOUND	MAKE A JOYFUL SOUND
AND DON'T BACK DOWN	
JUST STAND YOUR GROUND WHOO-HOO!	

(It ends in a huge flourish. CLAP-CLAP-CLAP!! The fear has been chased away. **MARION** *has buoyed everyone's spirits. She takes her bows, diggin' the adulation with both hands and a shovel.)*

DENISE. That was great Marion.

BELLE. You should be a singer.

*(***MARION*** *and* ***GERT*** *lock eyes. A secret they share.* ***GERT*** *nods support.)*

MARION. Really?

*(***MARION*** *looks down at the dress she's stuffed into and begins to ponder another path in life.)*

MARION. Well, maybe in another life.

(SALLY switches gears.)

SALLY. Come on, it's a dollar a point. Play.

(Fine. BELLE distractedly snaps up a card, barely even glances at it then sets down her hand. A nano-second later she picks it back up and –)

BELLE. Gin.

SALLY. What?

BELLE. Gin.

SALLY. You cheated!

BELLE. What?!

SALLY. You did. You cheated.

MARION. Sal!

SALLY. Forget it Marion. She's got sixty two dollars of mine. She cheated.

BELLE. I'm not the one that cheats people out of their money.

SALLY. I didn't cheat Westley –

BELLE. I saw him give you the money. I saw it. You are so jealous. *(She picks up the cards and makes them talk.)* I'm Sally, the queen of diamonds and I'm gonna destroy the Prince of Hearts so he can't be with the Queen of hearts anymore.

SALLY. *(Picking up the cards.)* I'm the Queen of hearts and I don't know jack.

BELLE. I'm the Queen of diamonds and all I care about is money. I'm bitter and cold and I'll be playing cards here when I'm old and ugly and alone. Long after Westley comes back –

SALLY. Oh grow up Belle! He ain't never comin' back!

(The room freezes. No one moves. You can hear heart-beats over the storm.)

BELLE. You're just tryin' to be cruel.

SALLY. Face it. That gambler cut his losses and ran.

BELLE. He did not.

SALLY. Yeah, he did –

BELLE. Only cause you cheated him – -

SALLY. I didn't cheat –

BELLE. I saw him give you the money –

SALLY. He paid me to distract you! *(BELLE freezes in shock.)* He paid so he could make a clean getaway.

BELLE. That's not true. Is it Marion?

(MARION wants to answer, wants to reassure. But sometimes the best thing you can do...

Gulp. BELLE looks to DENISE. But DENISE can't meet her gaze. Answer enough. Answer enough for a weaker woman...)

BELLE. He'll be back. He will. He loves me.

(Holding on to as much dignity as she can, BELLE runs from the room. DENISE goes out after her. GERT sets down her quilting and tries to follow as well...)

LOUISE STYLES. Gertrude. Let her alone.

GERTIE. Mother, she needs –

LOUISE STYLES. Nothing from us. Pick up your quilting.

GERTIE. *(She's had enough.)* No. I don't even like quilting. It think it's... just stupid. *(LOUISE gasps.)*

HARD CORA. Gert, don't talk to your momma that way.

LOUISE STYLES. I don't need any help from you.

GERTIE. And I don't want to cook.

LOUISE STYLES. You don't mean that. *(GERT won't. Mom's hangin' on by her fingernails.)* You'll never get married.

GERTIE. Maybe I don't want that either.

LOUISE STYLES. How can you say that?

GERTIE. You tell me this, school tells me that. Everybody's tellin' me something. What about what I want?

LOUISE STYLES. Fine. What do you want? *(Long silence.)* See, you don't know. You're still a child. And that's your advantage. We can strike while you're still young. You don't want to be middle aged, forced to take the only offer to come along. Trying to be everything to him. Learn these things now, have your choice of men.

GERTIE. You're not everything to him mother.

LOUISE STYLES. This isn't about me, sweetheart.

GERTIE. You're not.

LOUISE STYLES. That's enough. Stop it.

GERTIE. Do you really think he plays cribbage Tuesdays and Thursdays?

(That stops her. **GERT***'s in it now, and she can't turn back.)*

LOUISE STYLES. Who?

GERTIE. Who do you know that plays cribbage Tuesdays and Thursdays?

LOUISE STYLES. A man is entitled to a night out with his friends. If he wants to gamble a little, that's fine. Even drink a bit.

GERTIE. He's not with his friends, mother. Where is he Marion?

(Suddenly **MARION** *finds something, anything interesting on the floor.* **GERT** *closes in on her.)*

MARION. How should I know, Gert?

GERTIE. She needs to know.

MARION. I can't do that.

GERTIE. Tell her.

MARION. Gert. There's something to be said for the sanctity of a secret.

GERTIE. She needs to know.

MARION. I gave him my word.

GERTIE. Either you break your word to him, or I'll break mine to you.

MARION. Gert, don't do this. *(But* **GERT** *won't budge.)* He's right here. Tuesdays and Thursdays. Last room at the top of the stairs.

LOUISE STYLES. That's your room. That's a lie. I don't believe it. He'll close this place down when he hears of this slander.

(And she goes right back to her quilting. Stubbornly. Nothing has changed. Or has it? **MARION** *is drilling dagger eyes into* **GERT**.*)*

MARION. You got a lot to learn. *(***GERT*** runs off. Then awkwardly to* **LOUISE**...*)* For whatever it's worth... he was a good tipper.

*(***MARION*** vanishes.* **LOUISE** *just stitches... stitches... stitches. It's* **CORA** *who steps forward and offers the bandanna from her pocket.* **LOUISE** *won't take it, won't look at it, won't move.* **CORA** *drops it on the floor in front of her. And there it sits.* **LOUISE** *just stitches... stitches...)*

Song - ***FIFTY TWO YEARS***

LOUISE STYLES.
HERE IN THE DARK
THINGS LOOK THE SAME
NOTHING IS DIFFERENT, NOTHING HAS CHANGED
NOTHING BUT GOSSIP, NOTHING BUT LIES
YOU CAN SEE THE TRUTH
IF YOU JUST CLOSE YOUR EYES
I'VE FOUGHT TOUGHER DEMONS DRANK
EMBITTERED TEARS
AND HELD MY HEAD HIGH FOR FIFTY TWO YEARS

FOR FIFTY TWO YEARS I'VE FACED SOME HARD
TRUTH
THERE'S NO WISHING STARS NO SWEET BIRD OF
YOUTH
YOU TAKE YOUR PLACE IN SOCIETY
FOLLOW TRADITION AND PROPRIETY
TILL YOU PUT ALL YOUR FAITH IN THE WAY THINGS
APPEAR
NOT WHAT YOU'VE BECOME AFTER FIFTY TWO YEARS

A KISS IN THE DARK
WAS ALL HENRY GAVE
WHISPERS AND SHADOWS ROUND THE LOVE THAT
WE MADE
THOUGHT IT ROMANTIC HE REJECTED THE LIGHT
BUT THERE WAS SO MUCH MORE

HE WAS BANNING FROM SIGHT
CAUSE YOUR EYES ARE WIDE OPEN WHEN YOU
ENTER HERE
COULD IT HAVE BEEN ME, AND MY FIFTY TWO YEARS

I TOED THE LINE I NEVER TOOK THE CHANCE
TO DREAM, TO CRY, TO LAUGH, TO SING TO DANCE

FOR FIFTY TWO YEARS I FOLLOWED THE RULES
HAS IT BEEN FOR NOTHING HAVE I PLAYED THE
FOOL
WAS IT A DREAM AND I AM DOOMED TO WAKE
FROM A COMFORTABLE NUMB TO NIGHTMARE'S
HEARTACHE
IF THE TRUTH THAT I CLING TO DEEP IN MY HEART
WON'T STAND THE DAYLIGHT, HOW CAN I STAY …
HERE IN THE DARK… HERE IN THE DARK… HERE IN
THE DARK

(FADE TO BLACK)

Scene 3

(The entire set shifts stage right. The door moves center stage and **MARTIN** *is standing there in tattered rags. The* **STAGEHAND** *is there holding a fan and blowing dust on* **MARTIN**. *The dead bartender does a double take as the* **STAGEHAND** *simulates the storm.)*

(Through this number **MARTIN** *strips out of his clothes. Under he has a skeleton body suit. You know the kind they use for Halloween costumes. He strips down to nothing as the storm eats away his body. He starts to sing a Tex Rittery lament.)*

MARTIN.

WAS A NASTY OL' VARMIT IF IT MOVED I WOULD HARM IT
    I WAS MEAN AS TWENTY COWPOKES
TOOK WHAT I WANTED WHO CARED IF I HAUNTED
    THE DREAMS OF INNOCENT FOLKS.

A VANISHING BREED
A MAVERICK MAN OF THE PLAINS
A VANISHING BREED
THEY TREMBLED IN FEAR AT MY NAME
I WORE A BLACK HAT ON MY HEAD I WORE A BLACK HEART ON MY SLEEVE
A VANISHING BREED

I WAS JUST GOIN' TO DO SOME OAT SOWIN'
AFTER ALL SHE'S ONLY A WHORE
SHE OVER REACTED MY SIX SHOOTER BLASTED
ME TO MY FINAL REWARD

A VANISHING BREED
WASTING AWAY IN THE WIND
A VANISHING BREED
I THOUGHT THAT I WAS THICK SKINNED
THE STORM JUST PEELED IT AWAY I'M SHRINKING DOWN BY DEGREES
I HAVEN'T THE HEART TO GO ON I LOST IT HERE IN THE BREEZE

HAVEN'T A LEG TO STAND ON NOW I AM QUITE LITERALLY
A VANISHING BREED

(As the set resets to center, our ever present friend Mister Wind has finally found his true voice. Suddenly a HUGE CRASH rips the room from somewhere above. A scream. A large chunk of plaster falls to the floor. Then **LOUISE STYLES** *comes charging in, her hair a tangled mess, a giant cut bleeding on her forehead. All that self assured confidence is gone. She's deep in panic mode. A few seconds later the gang starts to appear, screaming over the now howling wind.)*

LOUISE STYLES. It's coming down!

MARION. What is it? What's wrong?

LOUISE STYLES. We have to get out.

SALLY. Get out?

MARION. We cant' get out darlin'.

COOPER. What was that?

DENISE. Is everyone alright?

LOUISE STYLES. This whole building is coming down on us.

DENISE. Try and calm down. Tell us what happened.

LOUISE STYLES. I am telling you. Just listen!

SALLY. What was the crash?

GERTIE. Our bedroom window.

LOUISE STYLES. It came crashing in. It's too much, this place won't stay up. We'll all be buried in here. Buried alive.

(Everyone crowds **LOUISE**, *all talking at once.* **CORA** *enters –)*

HARD CORA. She's right. Wind took the shutter, glass, even the frame. It's rippin' that room up pretty good. We're gonna have to reboard that window. *(To* **COOPER**.*)* Tools in there.

COOPER. What are we going to use for wood?

DENISE. How about the bed slats.

HARD CORA. And the chairs.

GERTIE. What about the dressers?

LOUISE STYLES. And that hideous armoire.

HARD CORA. Anything we can find.

MARION. We'll work in teams. Cooper and Denise. Belle and Sally.

BELLE. I'm not working with her.

SALLY. I'm not workin' with her either.

BELLE. You're just sayin' it cause I said it. Copy cat.

SALLY. Am not.

BELLE. Are too.

MARION. Enough! Cooper and Sal, Denise and Belle. Okay?

SALLY. Fine.

BELLE. Are too.

MARION. Cora, you're with me. Let's go.

(And they pound up the stairs. **CORA** *hesitates long enough –)*

HARD CORA. Gert – ?

GERTIE. We'll be fine.

LOUISE STYLES. We will not be fine, Gertrude.

GERTIE. Mother, you need to calm down.

LOUISE STYLES. We have to run.

GERTIE. And go where?

LOUISE STYLES. Anywhere.

GERTIE. How 'bout Daddy's livery? Or his mercantile? Father's bank? Where can you run mother?

LOUISE STYLES. I don't want to be here anymore Gert.

(Wow, and that's the truth of it. This is no longer a conversation about architecture.)

GERTIE. I know. But it's the safest place.

LOUISE STYLES. It doesn't matter, don't you understand? It doesn't matter how strong you think it is. You can spend a lifetime building something and it will fall apart. *(Beat.)* Now I am leaving.

GERTIE. No, you can't.

LOUISE STYLES. Get out of my way.

GERTIE. For god's sake mother, don't be stupid! – *(Whap!* **LOUISE** *slaps her face.)*

LOUISE STYLES. Don't you talk to me that way. You are not your father!

(Both women stand frozen in shock. Then slowly **GERT** *raises a hand and touches her slapped cheek. Something snaps in* **LOUISE**. *What have I done?!)*

LOUISE STYLES. Oh Gert.

GERTIE. It's okay Momma.

LOUISE STYLES. No it's not. You shouldn't be… No woman should be… I didn't mean…

GERTIE. Articulate momma.

LOUISE STYLES. *(A tension laugh)* Oh Gert. How do I face tomorrow?

GERTIE. With your eyes open.

LOUISE STYLES. I don't like what I see. I think I preferred it in the dark.

GERTIE. But there are a million colors you're missing momma. You deserve more than black and white.

(A moment passes as **LOUISE** *begins to cry.* **GERT** *just cradles her. Roles have been reversed. Then the rest of the cast comes pounding down the stairs.)*

SALLY. Am not.

BELLE. Are too.

SALLY. Am not.

BELLE. Are too.

HARD CORA. We got a problem.

COOPER. This just now occurring to you?

HARD CORA. The main support beam on the north east corner is coming loose.

COOPER. We got a problem.

HARD CORA. We boarded up the door, but that room is a tornado. If that wind gets a toe hold underneath it, it's gonna lift the whole roof right off.

MARION. *(Coming down, hearing the last of this.)* Damn. Shoot. *(She almost whacks herself, then –)* Oh hell damn.

SALLY. Wait a sec. That's my room!

(She breaks for it. **BELLE** *stops her.)*

BELLE. You can't go up there.

SALLY. I got seven hundred fifty three dollars up there!

BELLE. You'll die up there.

SALLY. GET OUT OF MY WAY!

BELLE. NO! It's gone. It ain't coming back. Wake up. It's gone and you can never, ever get it back. *(A strange ironic empathy passes between these two.)*

SALLY. It's everything… Everything –

BELLE. No it's not. *(Awkward and loving hug.)* You've still got me.

SALLY. Oh GAWD!

GERTIE. Shouldn't we do something?

COOPER. No. We boarded the window. We've locked off the doors. We sit tight.

HARD CORA. No we don't. We go outside and chain down the gable or this whole place will come crashing down. It'll take us five minutes tops.

COOPER. That sand will take your skin off in five minutes.

HARD CORA. You don't know that.

COOPER. Look, you got no idea what you're up against here, little lady.

HARD CORA. Little lady?!

COOPER. That's a bonafide disaster out there –

HARD CORA. I know. I've been through one –

COOPER. You go out there and you're gonna do more than get your hair mussed and your dress dirty.

HARD CORA. Does it look like my dress?

COOPER. Look at you –

HARD CORA. *(Seething on overload.)* You're sayin' 'cause I'm a woman –

COOPER. That's real danger and I'm not going.

HARD CORA. There's a big surprise.

COOPER. What's that mean?

HARD CORA. Figure it out. Fryin' pan's in the fire and where are the men? Once again I'm in it alone. I'll handle it.

COOPER. You're a fool.

HARD CORA. Least I ain't a coward –

DENISE. *(Peacemaking.)* We've locked off upstairs. We've done everything we safely can.

COOPER. Right. We just hunker down and wait it out. Everybody just settle down and take a deep breath.

*(***BELLE*** literally sucks a deep breath, her cheeks puffed wide. ***CORA*** heads to the bar.)*

HARD CORA. Mules. Cowboys and mules.

BELLE. *(Exhale)* It's okay Cora. He probably knows what he's doin'. *(Another gulp. Hold it. Exhale.)* You know what you're doing, don't you Marshall? *(Gasps.* ***COOPER*** *looks like he's been kicked. He glares at* ***BELLE*** *who's oblivious.)*

LOUISE STYLES. Marshall? Who's a Marshall?

BELLE. He is.

LOUISE STYLES. A United States Marshall?

BELLE. Yup.

COOPER. Actually, I'm out. Retired.

LOUISE STYLES. And where did you say you were from?

COOPER. I didn't.

BELLE. San Fancisco.

LOUISE STYLES. I remember reading about a Marshall from San Francisco. Perhaps you knew him.

COOPER. Doubt it.

LOUISE STYLES. What was his name? Huckabee. "C" something. Conner… Cody… Cooper. That's it. Cooper Huckabee.

(All eyes drill into ***COOPER***. *They know it's him. He tries to cover –)*

COOPER. What?

LOUISE STYLES. You're a coward.

DENISE. What?

BELLE. She said he's a coward.

SALLY. Shut up Belle.

LOUISE STYLES. It was in all the papers. Came down through the telegraph. San Francisco territory Marshall Huckabee abandon his post and ran. Turned coward.

SALLY. Well that explains a lot of what's been happening.

DENISE. Is that true?

COOPER. It's not that simple.

DENISE. You are or you're not.

COOPER. That's it? The day I became a Marshall I stopped being anything else. So now I'm a hero or a coward? For every five men I put away, five more would take their place. Then five more, and five more. Pretty soon I was lookin' over my shoulder, flinching at every shadow and whisper. Wondering if this heartbeat was my last.

DENISE. So you just abandoned everybody who was counting on you?

COOPER. This isn't exactly the way I had it planned. I mean, there was supposed to be...

Song - MAN OF DESTINY

COOPER.

THERE WAS A MAN OF DESTINY –
CARVING A LEGEND FOR HIMSELF
HE'D WALK THE PATH GOD MAPPED FOR HIM
PLAY THE CARDS THAT HE'D BEEN DEALT

HE TOOK THE VOW AND PINNED THE STAR
FANNED A BURNIN' DESIRE
TO HAVE HIS PAGE IN HISTORY
HE'D FACE THE MUSIC AND THE FIRE

BUT HE WALKED THE PATH IN IMPOSTERS SHOES
HERO'S MASK TO HIDE THE LIE
AN ACTOR'S COSTUME STRETCHING TIGHT
GREW TO BIG AS TIME WENT BY

THE LEGEND BLOOMED THE MAN DID NOT
AND SHRUNK WITHIN THE IDOL'S SKIN
NO ONE SAW THE BOY INSIDE
WHEN THEY ALL LOOKED UP AT HIM.

(Now the lights come up on those posters of Gene and Roy. The unreachable cowboy heroes.)

THERE WAS A MAN OF DESTINY
    TRYING TO BE WHAT THEY WANTED TO SEE
A MASQUERADE OUT OF CONTROL,
    HE LOST HIMSELF WITHIN THE ROLE
THE MIRROR BECAME THE ENEMY
    'CAUSE THE IMAGINARY HERO IS SO MUCH
BETTER. . .   THAN ME.

HE'D FACE THE NIGHTMARES AND THE DAYS
DRINKING COURAGE BY THE GLASS
HOPING ONE DAY TO BE FREE
FROM THE MAN IN THE IRON MASK
A LEGEND BURNING BRIGHTLY
DIES IN GLORY'S BLAZE
THE MAN WANTS TO LIVE QUIETLY
LONG AFTER HIS GLORY DAYS

THERE WAS A MAN OF DESTINY
    TRYING TO BE WHAT HE THOUGHT HE SHOULD
BE
A MASQUERADE OUT OF CONTROL,
    HE LOST HIMSELF WITHIN THE ROLE
THE MIRROR BECAME AN ENEMY
CAUSE THE IMAGINARY HERO IS SO MUCH BETTER. . .
THAN ME. WHOA OH WHOA OH.

TIME HAS WIDENED THE MILE 'TWEEN THE DREAM
AND REALITY
I CAN NO LONGER RECONCILE
    THE MAN I AM WITH WHO I WANTED TO BE

(Now a new poster rolls out. A shadowed hero's face. MAN OF DESTINY is the movie title. See the hero. See the legend. It creeps up behind **COOPER** *and towers over him.)*

THERE WAS A MAN OF DESTINY,
    FINALLY UNDERSTOOD HE COULDN'T SUCCEED
HE THREW IN THE TOWEL, HUNG UP THE GUN
    RETIRED THE TIN, TRIED TO OUTRUN
    THE MIRROR BECAME THE ENEMY
CAUSE THE IMAGINARY HERO IS SO MUCH BETTER...
THAN ME. WHOA OH WHOA OH
THAN ME.

(The lights have irised down into a single spotlight. He simply walks out of it. The light stays. Illuminating nothing. A ghost. A nobody. Then in the dark he catches **DENISE***'s eye. They stare at each other from across the room. Long beat before –*

– the door bursts open. Sand and wind doing a full frontal attack. **CORA** *comes staggering in. She has time for –)*

LOUISE STYLES. Oh my lord!

GERTIE. Cora!?

LOUISE STYLES. What was she doing outside?

SALLY. Getting' the mail.

DENISE. *(Looking at* **COOPER***!)* She went to chain down the roof!

*(***COOPER** *goes running upstairs as they girls scoop* **CORA** *up and put her on the bar. They hover around* **CORA***, completely ignoring* **GERT***'s advice.)*

DENISE. How is she?

MARION. She doesn't look so good.

DENISE. How bad is it?

SALLY. Let's get her up on the bar.

DENISE. Cora? Cora, c'mon, wake up.

MARION. What do we do?

GERTIE. We need to elevate her legs, get the blood back to her heart.

BELLE. How bout a little whiskey?

MARION. Thanks Doll but I'm too upset.

BELLE. I mean for her.

SALLY. What for?

BELLE. Whiskey helps dull the pain.

SALLY. She's not in any pain.

GERTIE. We need blankets to keep her from going into shock.

BELLE. Whiskey helps you sleep.

SALLY. She's out cold.

BELLE. Alright fine. How bout some rum.

GERTIE. Get her legs up.

MARION. I think we should get her on the floor.

GERTIE. We need to elevate –

BELLE. Here Cora, drink a little of this.

GERTIE. LISTEN TO ME! *(Silence falls like a knife.)* We need to elevate her legs.

MARION. Are you sure?

GERTIE. *(Dead rock solid.)* I'm sure. We need to clean out these lacerations. Water. *(Everyone's too stunned to move.)* I need water.

MARION. *(Looking behind the bar.)* I think we're out.

LOUISE STYLES. *(Pulling out a flask.)* Oh here. *(Off their looks.)* Well I didn't know what I'd catch from you girls.

(So **GERT** *takes over, as a doctor, cleaning out the wound. ANOTHER HUGE CRASH.* **COOPER** *comes back down looking scared.* **DENISE** *meets him at the bottom of the steps.)*

DENISE. The roof?

*(***COOPER** *shakes his head.)*

DENISE. She didn't chain it down?

COOPER. No.

DENISE. But that's okay, right? We just hunker down here and we're safe. Right?

COOPER. I don't know.

DENISE. But you said –

COOPER. Don't listen to me. You can't count on me.

DENISE. But –

COOPER. I don't know if I said it cause I believe it, or because I'm –

DENISE. A coward?

COOPER. Sounds harsher when you say it.

DENISE. But you're not.

COOPER. You don't know.

DENISE. Oh yes I do. Because…   **COOPER.**

ONCE UPON A TIME	THERE WAS A DAY
I BELIVED IN FAIRY TALES	I PLAYED THE HERO
KNIGHTS WERE ALWAYS WHITE	THEN I RAN AWAY
BUT THAT'S NOT TRUE	
I SEE YOU STANDING HERE	COULD I EVER BE
AND READ THE PAGES OF MY HEART	THE MAN SHE THINKS SHE SEES
AND WONDER STILL	
COULD IT BE YOU.	

COOPER.   **DENISE.**

I'M NO HERO	I'M NO PRINCESS IN A TOWER
I'M NO SAVIOR	YOU SAVED WHAT'S BEST IN ME
I'M NO ANGEL	WITH YOUR LOVE I FLY AGAIN
	YOU SET MY SPIRIT FREE

DENISE.

ONCE UPON A TIME

COOPER.

CAN I BE WHAT YOU WANT?

    DENISE.

      I BELIEVED IN FAIRY TALES

        COOPER.

          CAN I BE WHAT YOU NEED

DENISE.

ANGLES HAD THEIR WINGS

COOPER.
CAN I MAKE YOUR

TOGETHER.
DREAMS COME TRUE

COOPER.
CAST THE BOOKS ASIDE

DENISE.
SEE YOURSELF IN MY EYES

  COOPER.
  CLOSE THIS CHAPTER OF MY LIFE

    DENISE.
    THE MAN THAT I RECOGNIZE

TOGETHER.
OUR TALE BEGINS WHEN I MET YOU. WHEN I MET YOU.

DENISE. You're trembling.

COOPER. So are you.

DENISE. Funny. Yesterday I was willing to die. Today I'm scared.

COOPER. I gotta go.

(He grabs a rope off the wall. Ties himself into it. It all happens so fast.)

COOPER. If I'm not back in five, no wait, three, okay two minutes, pull me in anyway.

DENISE. What are you doing?

COOPER. Got a date.

DENISE. What?

COOPER. Cora's right. I think we all die if I don't go.

DENISE. You could die if you do.

COOPER. Yeah that's the icky part. Ironic, ain't it. I finally found something I'm more afraid of. A life without you.

*(Without a word, **DENISE** kisses him. Soft. Pure.)*

DENISE. My hero.

*(**LOUISE** wraps **GERT**'s wedding quilt around **COOPER**. Some protection. One last look around before he heads outside. Dust and wind hammer through the door. It's hell out there. **DENISE** lets out the rope. The door closes with a THUMP.*

***MARION** pounds on the floor, picking up a dead serious beat. Time stretches. **MARION** starts to sing, slow and haunting.)*

MARION.

DANCE WITH THE DEVIL WHEN HELL COMES A CALLIN'

MARION, BELLE & SALLY. *(Picking up the beat. Stomping and hitting furniture.)*

WHISTLE IN THE DARK WHEN MIDNIGHT ROLLS AROUND.

DENISE. Fifteen seconds

MARION & CAST.

YOU GOTTA SING LIKE AN ANGEL ON THE EVE OF DESTRUCTION WHEN NIGHTMARESKNOCK ON YOUR DOOR.

DENISE. Thirty seconds!

CAST.

JUST STAND YOUR GROUND AND DON'T BACK DOWN MAKE A JOYFUL SOUND!

DENISE. Forty five seconds –

CAST.

AND DON'T BACK DOWN JUST STAND YOUR –

*(Boom, The door bursts open and **COOPER** staggers in and collapses. **DENISE** dotes over him....)*

DENISE. Did you get it?

COOPER. Yeah.

DENISE. Will it hold?

COOPER. I don't know.

(The wind RAGES.)

(SLOW FADE TO BLACK)

Scene 4

(In the darkness there is no more wind. In fact what we hear now is birds. Just a few, chirping mildly. The lights come up and the saloon is gone. We're outside. **COOP** *and* **CORA** *enter.* **CORA** *back in her jeans and bandaged across her face and hands.* **CORA** *looks to* **COOP** *and doesn't know what to say. Her mouth opens for a thank you. She just shrugs and punches him in the arm instead. It's enough.)*

(COOP *smiles, is about to punch her back, but opts to grab a hand and kiss it.* **CORA** *chuckles.)*

HARD CORA. Yeah. Yeah.

*(***COOP** *tries to pull away but* **CORA** *just kisses his hand back. He doesn't know what to do as* **DENISE** *comes enters.)*

DENISE. How is it out here?

COOPER. It's a real mess.

DENISE. How bad?

HARD CORA. The town is gone. Wiped clean. Like the hand of god swept down and scoured the place off the face of the planet and – oh hell, you know. This is the only building left standing in town.

DENISE. Anything out there that shouldn't be?

COOPER. If there was, the storm took it.

(Oh good. Relief. **GERT** *enters.)*

GERTIE. What about your place?

HARD CORA. I got an anvil and stove maybe I can salvage, but that's about it.

GERTIE. I'm sorry.

HARD CORA. Yeah.

*(***LOUISE** *enters with a suitcase.* **MARION** *enters, sees this and runs to help)*

MARION. Missus Styles. Can I give you hand?

LOUISE STYLES. I'm fine.

MARION. Is there anything I can do for you? Anything at all?

LOUISE STYLES. *(Surprised to find out...)* No... I actually think I'll be fine.

MARION. *(Impressed despite herself.)* I'll be damned.

(BELLE and SALLY enter, BELLE handing over a small money bag.)

BELLE. So I give you my money with this one time investment –

SALLY. You become the *very* silent partner in a great cash earning opportunity. We split fifty fifty. Minus a handling fee and administration costs.

BELLE. Okay. Partner. *(She beams. Sally isn't sure she likes the sound of that. Belle looks around.)* Well, looks like Martin's place is officially closed.

SALLY. Yeah. Guess we ain't whores no more.

DENISE. Then who are we?

(She sounds as lost an afraid as everyone else here. The entire casts exchanges eye-lock, wondering the same damn thing. Then it's COOPER who breaks into a smile. He turns to the audience...)

COOPER. And that is the million dollar question folks. And the answer... surprised the hell out of me.

(The others have drifted off stage, leaving COOPER and DENISE alone. He smiles at her, drops to one knee. This is a proposal folks. He looks into her eyes...)

Song - NOBODY (Reprise)

COOPER.

I'M JUST THE NAMELESS COWBOY OF THE OLD WILD WEST
A PHANTOM OF THE PLAINS
THE FACELESS STRANGER RIDING IN THE SUNSET
WITHOUT A WHISPER OF A NAME

DENISE.

> I DO-OOOOOOOOOO

> WE'LL BE LEGENDS OF THE FRONTIER
> A MYTH A FAIRY TALE

DENISE & COOPER.

> THE STAR CROSSED LOVERS
> WHO LET LOVE PREVAIL

> *(Now the rest of the cast reenter.)*

ALL.

> CAUSE WE ARE NOBODY
> NOT WHO I ONCE KNEW
> NOBODY
> WE FACE THE DAWN ANEW
> NOBODY
> NO PLACE LEFT TO HIDE
> NOBODY
> TIME FOR ME TO RIDE

> ON THE HORIZON THERE'S A SUNSET WAITING FOR
> ME
> GONNA SADDLE UP AND HIT THE GOLDEN PRAIRIE
> FINALLY ALONE I LIKE THE COMPANY
> AIN'T IT FUNNY AFTER ALL THIS TIME I'M NOBODY
> FINALLY ALONE I LIKE THE COMPANY
> AIN'T IT FUNNY AFTER ALL THIS TIME I'M NOBODY

> *(The song hits its climax and our gang stands ready to face the world.* **COOPER** *turns to the audience.)*

COOPER. There you have it, folks. That's our little once upon a time. Now you may wonder what happened to everybody. Well…

(The lights change to isolate each character as he talks about them.)

Mrs. Louise Styles went back to her husband. And wasn't he shocked. Rumor has it that Susan B. Anthony got some of her ideas from Mrs. Henry David Styles.

*(***LOUISE*** takes out and dons a VOTES FOR WOMEN banner.)*

Gertrude didn't go back to St. Catherine's. Instead, she enrolled in medical school. She became a hell of a veterinarian. She took care of all the animals on Cora's Double D ranch. Gert never married, but she and Cora stayed... close through the years.

(CORA and GERT very subtly hold hands. BELLE wanders in, trying not to look lost.)

Belle quit waitin' for Westley and went home to Georgia. She only got lost three times.

(SALLY is picking through the debris, trying to see what can be salvaged.)

Sally stayed in town. And went into business for herself. And made a fortune.

(She holds up an "S" in the same logo as MARTIN's "M" that hung over the bar.)

Marion headed east and began a singin' career under her real name. Candy Morrill. I know, go figure. Heard she sang for President Grover Cleveland once, although she refused to have a cigar in the oval office. Martin was still dead. And me? I was the lucky one. After all, it is a fairy tale folks. I got the "happily ever after."

(He and DENISE kiss while the music kicks into high gear)

COOPER.

WELL THAT'S OUR TALE THE STORY'S SPUN
TIME TO MOSEY HOME
WE HOPE WE LEFT YOU SMILIN'
WITH A WINK AND A SONG

YOU'LL FIND YOUR HORSES WAITIN'
OUT BY THE HITCHIN' POST
WE HAD OUR NANNIES HOOTED
BUT NOW IT'S TIME TO GO

ALL.

OOOOOOO – - OOOOOOO – – - OOOOOOOOOH

COOPER.	THE GIRLS.
SO GIDDYUP	GIDDYUP
YEEHAW	YEEHAW
TEXAS TWO STEP OUT THE DOOR	
AND IF THE SPIRIT MOVES YOU	MOVES YOU
COME ON BACK FOR MORE	
ON THE HORIZON THERE'S A SUNSET WAITIN' FOR YOU	
	ADIOS SO LONG
SOMEWHERE THE PRAIRIE IS WAITIN' TO RENDEZVOUS	
	GET YOUR DOGGIES ALONG
WE'RE GLAD THAT YOU COULD STAY AND BE OUR GUEST	
	WE MUST CONFESS
AND SHARE THE SPIRIT OF THE WEST	
	SPIRIT OF THE WEST
VIYA CONDIOSE ON YOUR QUEST	
	WISH YOU SUCCESS
AND SPREAD THE SPIRIT OF THE WEST	
	SPIRIT OF THE WEST

ALL.

AND WE HOPE YA KEEP THE SPIRIT OF THE WEST

(Big finish. Final pose. Lights out.)

(FINAL CURTAIN)

COSTUME PLOT

Part of the fun of this show is the wink-wink/nudge-nudge homage to the singing cowboy musicals of old. We're not creating a history lesson here, we're jumping back to the wild west that never was. That playground for Roy and Dale. For Gene and Champion. So all the costumes should have a hyper reality feel.

There's no such thing as too much fringe or sequins. Play this idea as much as your imagination and budget will allow. Sometimes a web search of Retro/Vintage Western Wear will give some great ideas. Also find inspiration in the fashion of Nudie Cohn, the Rhinestone Tailor. Here are some suggestions we've used in the past.

COOPER
Pants with fringe down the leg seams. Tucked inside the boots of course.
A variety of bright western shirts.
> Flowers, Thunderbirds, poker hands, etc.
>
> Fringe
>
> Yolks and cuffs

White hat of course.
Large and colorful bandana.
Holster with his six shooter

MARION
Saloon gal outfit. Revealing, but Dale Evans tasteful.
Fishnets.
Feathers and boas work well and set her apart from the other gals.

SALLY
Saloon dress. Black and red works well.
As does oriental adornment.
Chopsticks in her hair.
A collapsible fan.
A silk Chinese robe she can take on and off is effective.

BELLE
Saloon dress. Lots of fringe and lace.
The ultimate southern Belle is what we're after here.
 Perhaps a parasol.

DENISE
Saloon dress.

This outfit should be a counterpart to Cooper's costume.
In color, tone, style. They should match.
The moment the audience sees them together they should know they were meant to be.

HARD CORA
First scene she wears colorful longjohns to sleep in.
For daylight hours she's in the ultimate side-kick outfit.
Black jeans and boots.
A large red & white checked shirt.
A dirty cowboy hat with the front plastered straight up Andy Devine style.
Gingham hankie.
At the end of act one she will have raided Marion's closet.

> A saloon gals outfit
> Lots of feathers, lace and frills.

LOUISE STYLES
In the first scene, she and Gert should have matching long nighties and bonnets
After that she's in full town matron mode.
Severe colors. Long skirt.
Ruffled shirt. Vest. Jacket. Very little skin shows on Louise Styles.

GERTRUDE
After matching mom's nightie and bonnet.
Think school marm.
Long dress.
High collars.
Long sleeves with just enough ruffles.
At the end of act one she will be mimicking Hard Cora.

> Black jeans and boots.

A large red & white checked shirt.
A dirty cowboy hat with the front plastered straight up Andy Devine style.
Gingham hankie

MARTIN
A bartender's outfit.
Black jeans.
White shirt, with appropriate blood and bullet holes.
Bolo or string tie.
Garters on the sleeves.
Vest.
All of this over a skeleton costume. The costume should be "breakaway" so during the song Vanishing Breed, the costume is stripped away and all that's left of Martin is bones.

PROP LIST

Dust is almost another character in this play. Except for the last scene, each time the door opens dust and wind should hammer through the door. Flour or corn meal works well. We don't suggest using sawdust or anything non-organic in case it blows in the actor's eyes or mouths. Good rule of thumb, if you can eat it, it'll work well. Sprinkle this mixture in front of an offstage fan and you've got instant dust storm.

Some props are set from the rise of curtain.

Canteen – on bar
Spittoon.
Whiskey bottles – behind bar or on shelves
Shot and drinking glasses – behind bar
Coffee mugs – behind bar
Breakaway bottle – behind bar.
Bar rags.
Rope to hold door closed.

Other props are brought on as needed.

COOPER
Saddlebags.
Gun.
Silver coin
Guitar that matches his outfit.
Book
Playing cards
Money
Book
Whiskey Bottle
Tool box with hammers and saw

MARION
Gun
Coffee pot
50 feet of rope
Suitcase

SALLY
Frying pan
Money
Playing cards
Boot
Knife
Blankets

BELLE
Writing pad and pen
Blankets
Money
Tattered dress
Hair comb

DENISE
Books
Suitcase

HARD CORA
Pocket knife
Chewin' tobacco (shredded jerky works well.)
Whiskey bottle
Messy lookin' quilt
Heavy chain

LOUISE STYLES
Quilt
Quilting needle
Flask

GERTRUDE
Whiskey bottle
Quilt
Quilting needle

SET DESIGN

The set is your typical wild west saloon. Singing Cowboy style. Lots of color. The hint of brick should be seen somewhere so we know why this is the only building in town that can withstand the storm. During act two we go "upstairs" for a while. What we have done is struck the bar and stools and used the upper platform for the upstairs area. Two freestanding doors and a lounge in each area set the scene. Lighting switching between upstairs and down can also help delineate between the areas. Below is a set design we've used in the past.

LIGHTING DESIGN

Lighting should be bright and colorful. Although most of the singing cowboys movies were black and white, we're bringing them into Technicolor. After the opening number the set should be dark and shadowed as Cooper stumbles in out of the dust.

Separating the lighting from "upstairs" and "downstairs" can really help during Act 2 Scene 2.

During the song Colors Of My World, feel free to go nuts with color. Let the set become even more alive as Gert starts to realize the colors in her world.

For Man Of Destiny we've discovered a haunting technique is to slowly fade the lights and let Cooper finish the song in a single overhead spot, turning him into a shadow of a man. A faceless silhouette. Pretty cool stuff.

SOUND DESIGN

Wind is our constant companion in this show. It never really vanishes until the final scene. It should rise, build and fall as the tension needs, but it is always nearby. A few recorded crashes as well as some live crash-boxes off stage will help sell the idea that the building is coming down around us.

Wild Dust The Musical Set Design

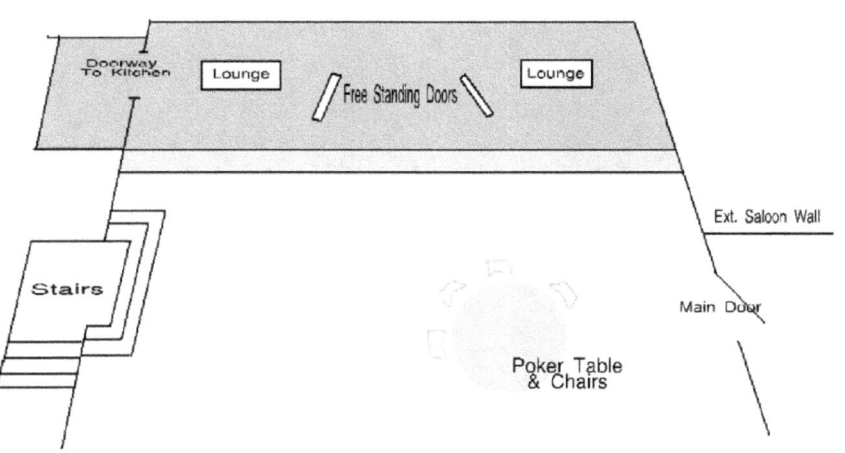

Wild Dust The Musical Set Design Act 2 Scene 2